NORTH SUN
or
The VOYAGE of the
WHALESHIP *ESTHER*

NORTH SUN

or

The VOYAGE of the WHALESHIP *ESTHER*

A Novel

ETHAN RUTHERFORD

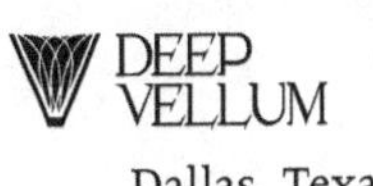

Published by A Strange Object, an imprint of Deep Vellum
3000 Commerce Street, Dallas, Texas 75226
deepvellum.org | @deepvellum

Deep Vellum is a 501(c)(3) nonprofit literary arts organization founded in 2013 with the mission to bring the world into conversation through literature.

Support for this publication has been provided in part by grants from the National Endowment for the Arts, the Texas Commission on the Arts, the City of Dallas Office of Arts and Culture, the Communities Foundation of Texas, and the Addy Foundation.

Library of Congress Cataloging-in-Publication Data

Names: Rutherford, Ethan, author.
Title: North sun, or, The voyage of the whaleship Esther : a novel / Ethan Rutherford.
Other titles: Voyage of the whaleship Esther
Description: Dallas, Texas : Deep Vellum ; Austin, Texas : /A Strange Object, 2025.
Identifiers: LCCN 2024035808 (print) | LCCN 2024035809 (ebook) | ISBN 9781646053582 (trade paperback) | ISBN 9781646053704 (ebook)
Subjects: LCSH: Whaling ships—Fiction. | Whaling—Fiction. | LCGFT: Sea fiction. | Action and adventure fiction. | Ecofiction. | Novels.
Classification: LCC PS3618.U7785 N67 2025 (print) | LCC PS3618.U7785 (ebook) | DDC 813/.6—dc23/eng/20240820
LC record available at https://lccn.loc.gov/2024035808
LC ebook record available at https://lccn.loc.gov/2024035809

Cover design and frontispiece by In-House International
Interior design and layout by Amber Morena
Printed in Canada

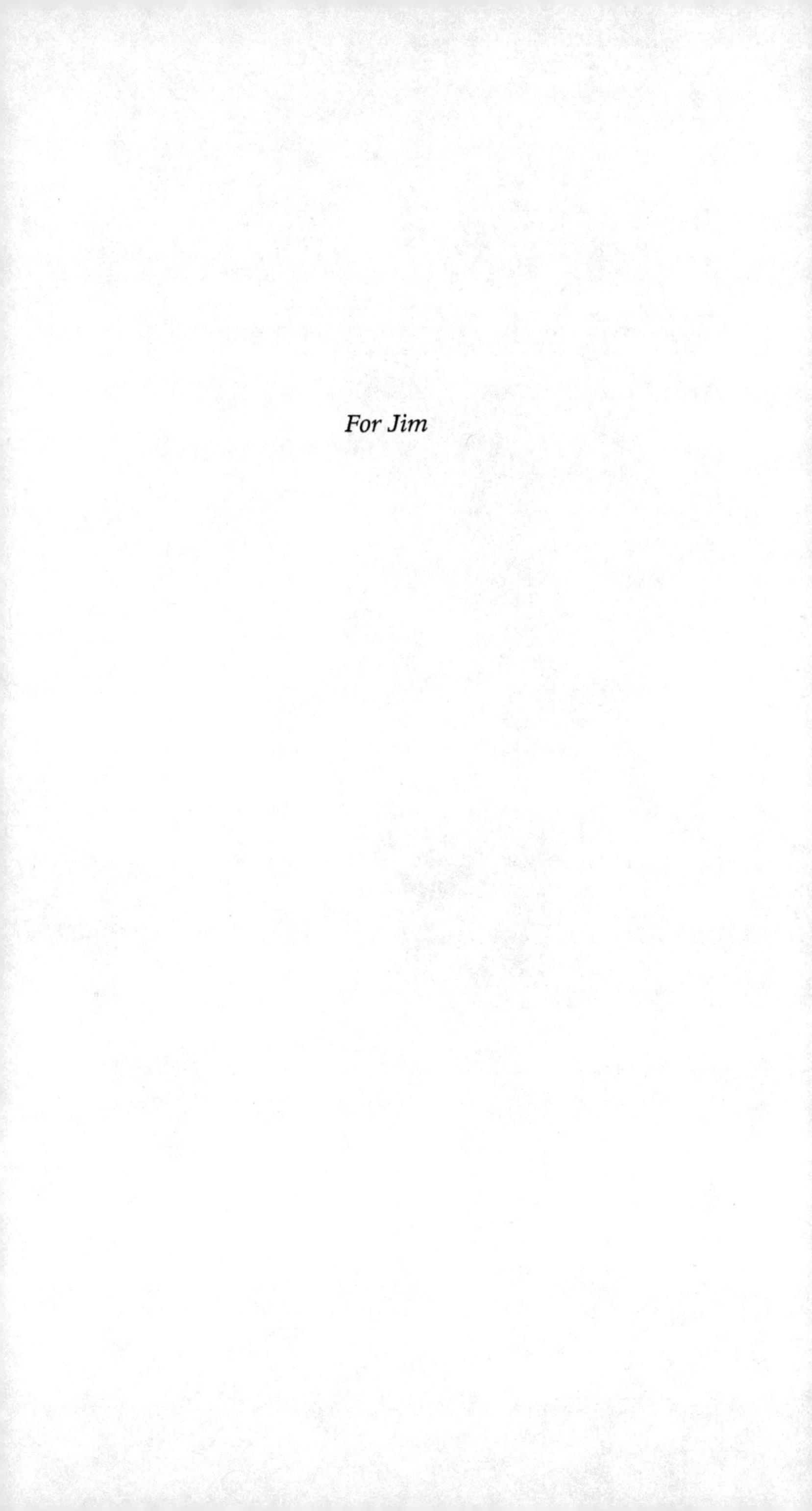

For Jim

The amiable Dr Adams suggested that God was
infinitely good.

JOHNSON: That he is infinitely good, as far as the
perfection of his nature will allow, I certainly believe;
but it is necessary for the good upon the whole, that
individuals should be punished. As to an *individual*,
therefore, he is not infinitely good; and as I cannot
be *sure* that I have fulfilled the conditions on which
salvation is granted, I am afraid I may be one of those
who shall be damned.

DR. ADAMS: What do you mean by damned?

JAMES BOSWELL, *Life of Johnson*

Listen, in some countries you kill a monster when
it's born. Other places, you kill it only when it kills
something else. Other places, you let it go, out into
the forest or the sea, and it lives there forever, calling
for others of its kind. *Listen to me*, it cries. Maybe it's
just alone.

MARIA DAHVANA HEADLEY, *The Mere Wife*

Many strange waves lifted and kicked their way into this novel as I was writing it, and though *North Sun* is wholly a work of fiction, the *Esther* would never have embarked if not for the inspiration and crucial information drawn from the following texts: *The Sea Voyage Narrative* by Robert Foulke; *Men and Whales* by Richard Ellis; *Whales, Ice, and Men: The History of Whaling in the Western Arctic* by John R. Bockstoce; *Following the Sea: A Young Sailor's Account of the Seafaring Life in the Mid-1800s* by Benjamin Doane; *Folklore and the Sea* by Horace Beck; *Harpoons and Other Whalecraft* by Thomas G. Lytle; *The Yankee Whaler* by Clifford W. Ashley; *Oil and Ice: A Story of Arctic Disaster and the Rise and Fall of America's Last Whaling*

Dynasty by Peter Nichols; *The Hunted Whale* by James McGuane; the photographs of Renate Aller collected in *Oceanscapes: One View, Ten Years*; the album *Ocean Songs* by the Dirty Three; *Drawing Restraint 2* by Matthew Barney; *The Oxford Book of Death*, edited by D. J. Enright; and *Into the Silent Land: The Practice of Contemplation* by Martin Laird.

Old Sorrel and Ashley himself are, to some degree, cento-esque characters, vessels themselves, and at various points in this novel they reference (and in some places, quote directly) the wisdom and work of others. In his conversations with the boys, Old Sorrel muddily alights on Samuel Johnson, Epictetus, the Longer Sukhāvatīvyūha Sūtra, and the Buddhist conception of Hell. In his final speech, Ashley's partial recitation is from *The Pilgrim's Progress* and the writing of William Scoresby. I aimed for accuracy on the water, but there are more than a few improbabilities in the *Esther*'s route, design, and hunt. These are intentional. This is a dream voyage, and at times the book tacked where she wished.

PART
ONE

New Bedford, Azores, Atlantic Ocean, Cape Horn,

South Pacific, Northwestern Grounds

\\\

The Letter, A Hospitable Ship, The Empty Archipelago,

First Whale, An Unexpected Visitor, A Fall from the

Hoops, Burial at Sea, Eastman Appears,

A Storm, Old Sorrel

\\\

1878

ONE

1.

Heavenly days! Behold!

The letter is in Arnold Lovejoy's breast pocket, and he taps it as he makes his way through the narrow streets of New Bedford and up to the big houses that overlook the harbor. He walks by the counting house, the chapel, the Chest of Arms. Tired women carrying full sacks of laundry pass him in the flat light of the morning.

At the empty center of town, he sits and lights his pipe. Some distance away, he watches a group of dirty children encircle a dog and prepare to torture it. One of the wretched boys calls the dog's name, Timbo, Timbo, while another ties his tail with a line attached to a large stick.

This isn't a game Arnold Lovejoy is familiar with or thinks he had the stomach for. He stands and wipes the tobacco flakes from his pantlegs. He is thirty-nine years old, stout and square-bearded, weather-faced from salt-spray, going gray at the temples like his own father had. He has just set foot on land, and already wishes to leave.

The dog yelps. Lovejoy doesn't linger.

2.

The letter he carries is dated March 1878 and brings the news that there is nothing to be done: the whaleship *Dromo* has been crushed by the ice in the Chukchi Sea. Her half-full cargo had been unloaded and stored ashore; her masts chopped; her iron instruments used for trading. Her ship's log remains with her captain, Benjamin Leander, who himself has stayed north. This letter informs the *Dromo*'s owners of the loss and of Leander's intention to stay where he is and never return.

These are dim days for the leviathan merchants. The smart whaling families have diversified and will hang onto their wealth for years to come. They've bought property in New York, invested in Pennsylvanian land to cash in on petroleum extraction, or else turned to banking.

The less smart, those convulsed by the strange desire to continue doing what had always been done, who consider it a divinely issued directive to rid the waves of great fish, now face a problem: the Atlantic whale that built their houses and ships has seemingly wised up, and anyone wishing to head out to sea to make a living looks at an Arctic voyage of three or five or sometimes seven years before the mast.

Such owners are the Ashleys.
The *Dromo* had been their ship.

3.

He, himself, has just returned from captaining a three-year expedition during which they'd taken and rendered less than a quarter of the anticipated fish.

How could it be? Only six years earlier, he'd stood at the helm of the *Sophie* and watched the Japanese waters roil and foam. They'd hunted and rendered so many; the sea was alive with families of whales. They'd turned the bay red and still found more to kill. This time, they'd hauled nearly nothing. His crew was surly and incompetent; they'd knocked into ice cakes and almost stove their own ship. Once north, they'd been so beset by an unrelenting fog that searching for bowhead had been a dreadful exercise. There were no whales anywhere that he, nor anyone else, could see. Other ships found them, but he did not.

To a man they were cold and wet and miserable. Upon landing in New Bedford, his crew took to the docks like scrambling rats, for with the short lay and what they'd slopped over the course of the *Sophie*'s voyage, and for all their hard work and time aboard, they found they owed money to the outfit. This failure felt terrible. The ice had joined Arnold Lovejoy in dreams and trailed him all the way home.

4.

Rounding a last corner, now a wide street. Setting foot on this lane is like opening the doors to a quiet shop where one has no business. The homes are Victorian. The hedges trimmed and boxed.

These grand and sturdy houses face the wharves and look like stern faces themselves. From the third-floor windows, which are the face's eyes, successful shipowners may sit and survey their fortune being built right in front of them. For years they've watched from this high perch, satisfied, as barrels and barrels of oil are rolled from each returning vessel and set on the wharves, or warmed their hands as their ships were heaved over and recaulked and sheathed and prepared for yet another voyage. At least, that's how it had been.

At a house unlike the others, Arnold Lovejoy stops to adjust his shirt. He checks the address on the letter. He knocks.

5.

He is received at the door by a stout woman in a black woolen overcoat, who, without a word, leads him through a dark and gloomy foyer and sits him in the library. In this room, all the shades are drawn. The walls are decorated with paintings of ships and scenes of the chase. *Flensing Among Floes; Spouting Off Larboard; The Cutting Party.* In one particularly gruesome illustration, two men prick at a large walrus with cutting spades while a third hoists what appears to be a large golden egg above his head. He looks more closely. It isn't an egg, exactly.

The walrus wears an expression of deep discomfort.

Directly above the fireplace, centered over the mantle, hangs a portrait of a young boy in a lime-green hunting coat. In one hand he holds a bugle. In the other, a small dog whose mashed face seems drawn out of proportion. The books on the shelves are histories of the Ashley family.

"Your frown," says Arnold Lovejoy, to the woman who has come and gone with his letter and now sits silently across from him, "is like a symbol in some long-lost alphabet."

She makes no reply. At the sound of a bell, she turns and walks out of the room, summoning him; he stands and follows. There are no rugs on the floor, nor any wall decoration, but he knows the woman's coat is made of the finest wool and the wooden floor planks are pine.

A flensing pole leans comfortably in the corner of the staircase.

6.

The curtains in this wide sitting room are drawn as well, and on one table someone has spread a map. The whole place is candlelit; even the dark corners are cast in a fine light. In front of Arnold Lovejoy sits a small man with no hair and a woman with sharp teeth. Ashley himself, and to his left, his wife. "Captain Lovejoy," says Ashley. "Thank you for delivering your letter. Or, I should say, my letter. The *Dromo* was my favorite ship. I'm sorry she's been lost."

"Very sorry," says Mrs. Ashley.

They are not really monsters, Arnold Lovejoy knows. They just appear that way. It's in their blood.

"For nearly a year I've sat in disquiet, eager for news of my ship. What's happened to her, I wondered? I know now. And in that time, in this room, waiting off the water for so long, I've developed a strange craving. Not for foul duff, of course—foul. I'm speaking of salt horse, that special treat of the sea. You don't have any, do you? At your age, I carried a strip in my breast pocket, which made me a friend to all dogs ashore I can tell you. They followed me all over town. With them I behaved admirably, I gave them licks. It's nothing to be nervous about, if you don't have one, you don't, but I thought perhaps you were like me, and carried a strip in your breast pocket, like a memory of the sea itself. I ask every returning ship, and every returning captain who darkens my door. No? Very well.

"Come closer. Use your imagination: receive a strip from my hand. The proper way to wash it down is with water, sometimes after soaking it. Always, my favorite pieces were gamey ones, ones that no one else wanted. I chose them to be virtuous, but soon came to like the taste, and whenever I saw a piece that had been passed over two or three times by the crew, my mouth would go numb—my piece.

"Some men grow to hate the meat. But that's the same as saying you hate the sea, and your ship, and your captain, and everything you've decided to do with your life. . . . Now, chew. It's the fibers. They untwine in your mouth, and some lodge near your gums between your back teeth . . . I don't have those teeth any longer of course, this was years ago! But don't the years pass like days. This is always a double pleasure for me. First, to eat the meat, which is making me salivate as I speak to you now; then the pleasure of feeling a slight discomfort in your gums as you fall asleep; then further pleasure, as often the next evening as the next morning, when you relentlessly tongue the fibers and snag them, and they are finally released from their hiding place to drop back to your mouth. It was all we ate on my ships. It cost me no money at all. Some ships I knew caught and ate seal, but I myself have no taste for that tricky creature. Men who eat seal are not normal afterward. They open themselves up to nightmare."

"That's . . . ridiculous," says Mrs. Ashley.

Ashley himself frowns. "Not at all."

8.

"Tell us about Benjamin," Mrs. Ashley says. "Leander, I should say. How did you come to have this letter?" Arnold Lovejoy coughs and speaks: "That was not the name he gave. In fact, he gave me no name at all. He said he'd been without his ship for months. He was wearing skins. He was alone on the ice. We were on our way out, and he asked me to deliver it to you."

"Did you read the letter?" "Of course not." "Did you invite him aboard?" "Oh, yes," says Arnold Lovejoy. "He had no interest."

"Did he ask you to deliver anything else?"

Pause. "No."

"You realize he lives in the palace of his mind," says Mrs. Ashley.

"I did not note that," says Lovejoy.

"He always has."

9.

In the silence that follows, Arnold Lovejoy feels as though he is sitting for a painting, lightheaded; he thinks he might leave his feet. In his hand, he still holds the imaginary piece of salt horse given to him; he places it in his pocket. He looks at the Ashley crest over the fireplace: a darting knot above three whales.

Overcome, he kneels.

"My father was a whaleman," he says. "Our family has always admired yours. He is dead now. But he would be proud to see me here." "How polite," says Mrs. Ashley. He can think of nothing else to say. "How long ago?" "Ma'am?"

"Did he die."

"I find I can't remember, exactly. It's been years. Years and years."

He had met the Ashleys once before. He'd been clean-shaven then, and young, at his father's side, in this very room. And though their history on the water was indelible to him, he hadn't expected to be remembered, for the Ashleys were famous and known to all good men of the sea. Revered around New Bedford, they had built a formidable fleet of whaling ships and had taken over or put out of business all other candlemakers in southern Massachusetts. As businesspeople they were ruthless.

As whalers, they'd had no equal.

On land, they were known as much for their generosity to the town as they were for their inability to forgive a grievance. They seemed to luxuriate in them, Mrs. Ashley in particular. She was a stern woman, with a muster of gray, metallic hair that sat atop her head like a ball of thin yarn, through which her scalp was visible; her brow was perpetually creased.

She did not forget a slight—why should she? She'd accompanied her husband on his early voyages and had born him two sons and a daughter on the sea.

Not a single Ashley was over five feet tall.

The *Dromo* had been an Ashley bark seemingly for centuries and was famous herself in her own way: once she had been used to return runaway slaves from Massachusetts to Charleston.

"Here, now," says Ashley. With a sigh he stands, walks to still-kneeling Arnold Lovejoy, takes him by the arm, and lifts. "He can't stay on the ice like a madman. Surely you understand." His grip is viselike and cold.

He compels Arnold Lovejoy to a table piled high with careful maps, selects one, and flattens it.

The map is beautifully rendered. It looks like an ancient scroll and appears to glow in the candlelight as Ashley runs his fingers over the markings—ink dots indicating barrel amounts of a take, sightings, routes. This map is of the northern grounds, from where Arnold Lovejoy has just returned. In one corner is drawn a lifelike sawfish. In another, a fantastically rendered mermaid, with beautiful breasts and a seal's split tail.

"Point out where he was?" says Ashley.

As Arnold Lovejoy begins to explain—near St. Lawrence Island, slightly south, demoralized, unsure if they were seeing a man walking toward them over the ice or not—a small cry comes from behind one of the full-drawn curtains. He realizes that someone has been hiding there the whole time.

"Hush," says Mrs. Ashley.

Finally, Ashley rolls up the map, locks it away, and thanks him. He retrieves a small sack from his desk and presses it into Arnold Lovejoy's hands.

"Oh," says Arnold Lovejoy. "This is unnecessary."

"You haven't read by light until you've lit an Ashley

candle. Finest Sperm Candle. Drives the dark out, eliminates it, enfolds it, and kicks it outside. It's for thee. In thanks, in admiration, in pity. For the letter."

Arnold Lovejoy nods slowly, glances once at the curtain, and allows himself to be shown out by the dour, stout woman who had greeted him earlier with such misery. "Such a slaughterous age," says she. "One can't be sentimental. Still, I wish he'd come home. But he shan't, shan't, shan't."

12.

Well-known to all returning whalers is the Davit Inn, a tavern whose low-lit interior approximates a captain's quarters. Upon entering, Arnold Lovejoy is pleased to see that after all these years the owner still hangs sketched drawings of old wooden ships on his walls. He reads the ship and signal flags carefully pinned above the bar. House flags hung to summon the old grandeur of the sea. Smudge pots line the corner like squat, silent sentinels. No pictures of steamers allowed.

The bar itself is lit by lamplight.

The owner of this inn is famous. Everyone knows him—he is an old whaling captain himself. He would be, thinks Arnold Lovejoy, almost seventy years old. One son abandoned him and the family business in the search for gold in the western seams, the other had his head taken clean off by cannon fire at Antietam. But when, as Lovejoy sits, he asks after the owner by name, the barman behind the counter sucks his teeth.

Let it be, he thinks, and orders his rum with sugar.

Of the four other men in the bar, three have no nails on any finger save the thumb. They are old riggers and will not look at him. Their hands are ruined. They are cloaked in tatters and wear their canvas pants stained. They will never be on a ship again in the role they had become accustomed to.

"I have just been to the Ashleys," Lovejoy finally says.

"Not true," says the barman.

"Inside, even. Summoned."

"How was it?"

With a sip of his rum, he replies: "Magnificent."

So settled, the morning returns to him: the dour woman, the shut door, the quiet street. As he'd departed and walked down to the harbor, the Ashley's house had loomed behind him like a medieval castle, its twin widow's walks dipping below the trees, just out of sight. The visit had been short, but what had he expected? He had at the very least delivered the letter and shown the proper respect. As he turned another corner and the tavern came into view, he felt the day's silence swell through him.

Then the sun pulsed and pushed through the gray clouds like a vibrating eye.

"Excuse *me*," said some woman.

He'd been startled by a clattering sound. Looking up from the cobblestones where he'd been tracing his thoughts, he saw, caterwauling toward him, the sweet dog Timbo. He ran with his mouth open, his tongue lolling like a limp flag; he had no teeth. In a panic, he was trying to outpace the large stick tied to his mangy tail, yet no matter what he did, the stick pursued him with relentless malice. He turned in circles, he threw himself at a bush. It seemed he was on the verge of losing his mind. He hopped once, twice. Then he reached between his legs, caught his tail in his mouth, and bit until he howled.

This delighted the children, who had followed him for much of the morning in the hope of hearing such a sound.

One saw the end coming and hoped it wouldn't. His

work on the sea had always been brutal and lucrative for his ship's owners. But now the aperture had closed and gone dark, and embarking was like attaching a fresco to the inside of an eggshell.

"What is that, now?" says the barman.

"A candle," says Arnold Lovejoy. "The finest." He unwraps and sets it down on the bar. The cloth it's come in is embroidered: three whales, a darting knot above. He flattens the emblem carefully and studies it.

"Fearsome creatures," the barman says, and refills his drink.

Arnold Lovejoy nods.

Then he speaks.

13.

"To keep my sanity aboard the *Sophie*, I began to suspect there was a *reason* my men were not spotting whale and I felt it was my job to find out what that reason was. But I didn't. The *Sophie*'s voyage was drudgery, gross work for nothing. We lost two steerers in the black water. Not a single thing went right. Near the end, I began to feel as though my life on that cursed ship had all along been happening to another person, and I was in someone else's skull, looking out. Purest failure, of the purest sort. And now it is over. The *Sophie*'s debt is unconquerable. It is as though I have walked myself slowly into the darkest of caves, wet and cold, with no sounding equipment to help me out.

"My wife waits for me. My girls will be ten, now. Of them, I can recall very little. They were not present in my thoughts while I sailed. To think of them now—they are wisps of smoke. I attempt to grasp them, and I hold nothing. Perhaps I'm not trying hard enough. It's a bad feeling. I'm sure you've heard worse. But the sea is empty. That's what I have to tell you.

"Also this: years ago, sitting on this exact stool, I saw a man's throat slit, lobe to lobe. The poor man flopped on the floor, no head, or more precisely, his head half off his body. His attacker stood over him, yelling abuse until suddenly his own face went white—for he'd been sent to kill one man but, in error, snuck up on and killed an-

other. 'I would take it back if I could,' he said. He'd begun to cry. But he left and was not punished."

"I've heard that story," says the barman.
   "I am not normally so talkative."
   "Another?"
   Arnold Lovejoy signals, yes.

14.

By the time one of Ashley's sons tracks him down, Arnold Lovejoy is well into his rum and has talked his way into the company of the riggers.

They've lit the sperm candle and set it in the middle of their glass-strewn table; they watch it burn clean and bright all the way down. It really is the finest light, and bathed in it, the riggers look like young men again. They lean into the candle's glow and allow their thoughts to wander far and wide. "It's the end of the world up there," says one of the old riggers. "Ice, ice, ice." "The world's always ending somewhere," says another. The third old rigger clears his throat. "*A* world is always ending," he says. "Not *the*."

"Captain Lovejoy," the younger Ashley says. "That is not me," says Arnold Lovejoy. But the young man knows better.

"I have a proposal for you," he says. "It's one you will want to hear."

15.

"It is not true that all sailors are in love with the sea," says the younger Ashley, "but I can say with relative certainty that the captains of whaling ships do not thrive in retirement. Where once they conducted themselves with utmost assurance and autocracy, on land they are uncertain and lost. At sea, a captain is the center of his kingdom, his word is law—his crew look to him for guidance and reassurance and accept their punishment should it be necessary.

"On land, even the most wily captains, those on whom nothing regarding the salt sea is lost, and to whom whaling came easily, who never once returned home with a ship less than fully greased, who presided over the slaughter and trying out and chopping and bundling of bone, who asserted their will over the great beasts of the deep and did not flinch—on land they find a circuit of social obligations impossible to navigate. Offense is given and taken freely; one finds himself without a head for numbers; one understands the humiliation of poverty if he is that unlucky; one reaches for a wife only to get a cheek, a tentative yes, the dawning recognition in the eyes of his children that the great man they'd heard about, whom they dreamt was just over the watery horizon, is nothing more than an ordinary fool who walks with his head to the ground telling stories of the sea to anyone who will listen.

"A captain without a ship is a flightless bird. This is not to romanticize the profession, or to deem it a calling of the highest sort, only to state the obvious—that a man, when stripped of his utility, understands with a great shame just how unnecessary to the Earth's orbit he truly is. And what's left for him then? Perhaps only civility, servility, the dull path of law.

"It's tempting to think of our industry in toto as nothing more than a fleet of ships ridding the waves of whale, thinning their numbers, taking what the world's oceans provide and returning full-up with casks—in other words, an industry that grabs everything and gives nothing. But that would not be true. For it was the whaling ships which brought influenza, cholera, and tuberculosis to the Pacific Islands. Measles killed thirty thousand natives . . . I'm kidding, of course . . . I'm almost in tears . . .

"Leander is the husband to my only sister. He has scuttled the *Dromo*, a bark not his to scuttle, taken her valuables as his own, and forsaken all kindness shown to him by my parents and, I might add, myself. My sister is heartbroken, and her child is a frail creature . . . One of our ships is being outfitted on the wharves. Her name is the *Esther*. You've had bad luck, but it need not continue, for despite what you've seen and read in various reports spread by our newspapers like a virus, grotesquely, the ocean is *not* empty.

"Let me lay the proposition in your ear: take command of the *Esther* and make haste to the northern grounds where you received the letter. Find my brother-in-law and escort him home if he is so willing. And take as many whale as possible along the way."

"Is this a true proposition?" asks Lovejoy. "It is," says the younger Ashley. "It is redemption. It is, for you, a way forward. It is also a favor, asked. But it will make you rich." "Why me?" asks Arnold Lovejoy. The younger Ashley nods.

"Why not?"

17.

"The world gives itself over to those in our favor. Do you believe in such luck? Do you believe in continuity? Do you prefer interruption and whimsy? Do you dream of penury? I will dispense with the flattery. I have spoken to your wife, and she is indifferent to you. I have seen your children, and of you they have no solid memory, simply a feeling of warm abstraction, the saturated idea of a gone father. Perhaps these are relationships you could salvage. But you cannot do so as a farmer or as a tax collector, baker, butcher, soldier, spy. They do not wish to be poor.

"My father knows the owners of your last ship. Your debt is a problem; he can snap his fingers at it, and it will disappear. It is simply a matter of will. Yours." Snap. "This place is a theater of dreams. It already slips from memory." Snap. "The *Sophie*, a vision of failure, gone." Snap. "But allow me to draw your attention to something while we are here: these ships which hang on the wall. They are full-flagged ambassadors of reason and industry. And what wonderful names they had: the *Mary and Helen*; *Sunbeam*; *Amaret*; *Commodore Morris*; *Fame*. The *Halcyon* is right over there. She was the pride of Nantucket, a ship whose pure lines stopped sailors in their tracks. But she was sunk off the coast of Japan by the *Shenandoah*. My father is suing for that."

18.

The younger Ashley draws down his drink, and taps it, delicately, on Arnold Lovejoy's own.

Gazing at Ashley's son, the young man hadn't appeared to Lovejoy like his father, but as the eyes adjusted, he'd begun to look *exactly* like him. "Strange things *do* happen," the boy continues. "One day, you return home with nothing, and the next you are given the opportunity of a lifetime. Simply summon your will. The lay is one quarter. And if you return with my sister's husband, you will be paid even more handsomely. If you accept, there are a few more stipulations. But nothing major. We need your answer in one week."

He signals the barman and pays.

"Did you hear?" Arnold Lovejoy asks the barman when the boy has gone. "I did," the barman replies. "Not all of us live in such sunlight."

At home, Arnold Lovejoy finds neighbors who don't recognize him, a wife who won't touch him, and two children who, though fair and considerate, have not missed him at all. "Poor man, poor man," his animals say.

And what would his own father have thought?

He dreams he is still on the waves. Twice he is kicked in the chest by the horse who'd been given his name. His bedroom will not stop rocking back and forth. The tall trees make him feel ill, small and sad. One evening, after an argument, he forces the issue with his wife, slips his fingers in her, turns her over, and, though she is quiet and acquiesces, afterward she runs, sobbing angrily, out the kitchen door and into the forest.

His debts dance before his eyes like merry men. He entreats his wife and daughters to accompany him on the *Esther*; they demur. Yet he knows what he's been told is true.

The sea is calling.

It takes him four days to accept the Ashleys' offer.

TWO

20.

"The *Esther*," says the younger Ashley, "is a bark-rigged schooner, oak-ribbed, tub-bottomed, made from the finest material—her hull is finished with yellow pine and copper-sheathed.

"As you'll see, she's not a fast ship, but in her long and difficult life, she's neither sagged nor hogged, and not much else can be asked of a whaling vessel of her stature. We are proud to say her tryworks have never been broken down; they sit midship and retain their original Ashley imprint. The only aspect of her appearance that might be held against her is not her fault: during the war, she was painted with false gunports at the waterline, and we have not painted them over."

At the dock, Arnold Lovejoy is pleased to see the entire waterfront organized around attending to the *Esther*'s needs as though courting her favor. He counts five men shaving and resheathing her hull; a steward calling as he marks and stows arriving supplies—staves, headings, hoops, iron. By midmorning tomorrow, her crew will be assembled: first mate, second mate, third mate, and three boat steerers; a blacksmith; a cooper; a cook; thirteen seamen; and two boys. Even on her lines, as now, one knew this beautiful ship would not go tubs up if caught in a typhoon or harassed by a whale.

His own quarters are lush and more spacious than he'd

enjoyed aboard the *Sophie*. Near his bed is a navigation table, a dining nook, and a commode.

The bed itself is on gimbals.

"You'll come to the dinner?" asks the younger Ashley once they've walked the deck. "Oh, yes," Arnold Lovejoy replies.

"Tonight."

"Of course."

21.

That evening, as the younger Ashley escorts Arnold Lovejoy through his father's elegant dark hallways, he points and speaks: Here is a painting of my father, at ease atop the spotting nest; over here my mother, and behind her the sea. This is me, as a child, clad in sealskin. And this is my sister, Sarah, holding in her lap an etching of the hatless man, one of the treasures sunk with the *Dromo*.

"And who is this?"

"Edmund Thule, in his younger days. You will meet him, he will be with you, a small stipulation." Arnold Lovejoy looks closer at the canvas: pigment, shade, but the figure doesn't fully cohere. "He's older now," says the younger Ashley. "He will introduce himself and sleep aft in his own quarters. He's not to be included in normal duty until you reach the ice. You've travelled with passengers before?"

"Many times," says Lovejoy.

"He will give you no trouble," says the boy. "In fact, it's likely you won't see much of him at all. He has been attached to many of our expeditions." Near the end of the hall, a spot on the wall where a portrait once hung. "That was Leander. We've taken it down until he returns."

The double-flue harpoon in the corner. "And we've arrived," says the younger Ashley.

22.

Ornate chandeliers bathe the great room in candlelight.

A feast of fish and fowl has been lain beautifully, ringed by heaps of crimson crab. It seems everyone in New Bedford is in attendance. Guests smile and lift hands in a dance Arnold Lovejoy can neither follow nor participate. He doesn't mind, for it is to him everyone wishes to speak. On his third rum and sugar, he gives instructions to an elderly couple about how to properly scoop the headcase of a sperm whale. On his fourth, he regales a group of children with stories of cannibals. Every story meets with admiration, each affirming glance leaves him lighter on his feet. He loses the younger Ashley in the crowd, finds him, loses him again. He eats from overflowing plates, and drinks from goblets. "Welcome, welcome, welcome," calls Ashley himself. "We are all hungry and eager!"

"Eat, mingle, make merry!"

Over the course of the evening, he spots:

A group of cloak-clad men, huddling near the fire; the old riggers from the Davit Inn; a bear's head, mounted with his teeth filed, hung high on the wall. A man dressed in flowers, who appears and offers him another drink. "Why not?" says Arnold Lovejoy. "Why not," the man says.

He has never felt so appreciated, nor so perceived. He drinks what is offered. In the quivering light, the paintings seem to come alive on the walls. From the house's window, he spots the mooring lanterns of ships in the harbor; the break on the jetty; and beyond that the dark, delectable sea.

And then into his vision walks the most beautiful woman he's ever seen. "Captain Lovejoy," she says. Her eyes are like blue glass set gently in the most delicate porcelain. She has materialized it seems from the air itself. "I am Sarah Ashley." The whole party organizes itself around the two of them. She looks nothing like the portrait hanging in the hall. "Tell me what is missing," she says.

23.

In the sudden quiet, he feels compelled to speak.

It is though someone else were speaking. He tells of meeting her husband and receiving the letter—a tall man, seemingly in good health, who appeared on the ice as though cut from fog. A balaclava so encrusted with rime his face was obscured: he could've worn a beard, or not. "I did not see him perfectly," he says. "Though he would not come aboard, we did give him a tin of fish. He blessed our boat and waved farewell."

Her expression is unreadable.

24.

"You have left your family, too. This is a story itself."

"It is," says Lovejoy. "I asked them to come with me. But there is no other way."

The partygoers near them quiet like a congregation hushed.

She smiles. "There is no other way," she repeats.

Into his open palm she places a small, wrapped package. She holds his hand and closes his fingers around the gift. His eyes fix on the near distance. As she speaks, she is sound itself. "When you see Leander, show this to him. It binds you to me and will return itself home."

"You must hold in your mind that he wishes to return. You must remind him of me and of our child and help him understand what he has done. He holds in his possession something that does not belong to him. It has guided the *Dromo*; it will, in time, pull you to him and bring you home. It is this you must also retrieve and return to me. I wish you an easy passage, but you must expect hardship and meet it with courage. This gift of mine will help you. The voyage is long, yet it may feel as though no time is passing. You will encounter great and many challenges; in facing them, you must be resolved. The whales will come, but do not seek hazard; bring the *Esther* to the ice and safely back. He waits for you. As, in prudence, will I."

On her neck he smells ambergris and lavender.

Close, now. Into his ear, she whispers: it had been she behind the curtain during his visit.

"Be swift, be careful, be true!"

26.

The party, remembering itself, regains its speed and whirling strength. He clutches the package to his chest until she turns away. The crowd comes back to life, opens its gullet to swallow her, and he sees her no more.

"Goodbye," Ashley himself says.

"Farewell," says Mrs. Ashley, and kisses his hand.

"Good luck," says their son, who has escorted him to the door of their grand house and shuts it behind him.

Into the dark of night, he walks. On his way down to the harbor, the trees become people. The buildings, fluking whales. He sees, in his hand, a gilded lance. As a child, he had known the Ashley barks by their color and flag: a darting knot above three whales, set on green tapestry, sewn into canvas. Beautiful ships, they never sank. They were perfect: slaughterous tubs, slow cookhouses, patient, patient, patient. They always came home, long a point of pride. His pride, their pride; it was one in the same. "She feels no pain," his father would say in admiration, as one or another returned to the harbor he sees now. "Look at those lines! Watch how heavy she sits!" Heavy meant full: barrels and barrels to the bursting.

His, now.

"Pride." The full moon hangs in the sky like a luminous skull. She sweet-talks him to the wharves, past the barrels, the baleen bundled and stacked, up the gangway, to the *Esther*. "Arnold Lovejoy," says the man sitting in his cabin.

"I am Edmund Thule."

28.

"I didn't mean to startle you. Please sit."

Edmund Thule's face is shaped poorly in the lantern-light, underlit, large-chinned, and, to Arnold Lovejoy, his appearance is like that of a greyhound: thin lips, and small, unblinking eyes. "I've been at the Ashleys'."

"I've been waiting here," says Thule.

"What do you have?"

He sets the wrapped package on his captain's table and slowly hangs his weather jacket near the door. With a knife retrieved from his navigation chest, he gently cuts the twine, opens the charts that serve as wrapping, and brings the lantern near. It's a tooth from a sperm whale, yellowed and smooth, nearly as large as his forearm.

On one side he sees a careful etching of Sarah, herself—her clothed shoulders and delicate face set in a circular frame. On the other is the Ashley imprint, a darting knot above three whales. Below is written in bone: Endurance, Abundance, Safety at Sea. "It is a present from Sarah Ashley. I am to give it to Leander." "Ah," says Thule. "I would hang onto that."

"I aim to," he replies.

29.

Their conversation is not long and seems, in part, a whispered thing.

As a passenger, Thule will stay below, out of the way and sight, in his own cabin. Though he has sailed for years under various Ashleys and will serve as a listening ear to Lovejoy in his captain's quarters, he is not to be bothered by the crew, nor included in any of the *Esther*'s normal duty as they hunt and tack. "When we get to the ice, I will accompany you in your search for Leander. I know him well, and he will be pleased to see me." "How pleased?" "Visibly," says Thule. He stands to leave.

"Undoubtably." He shuts the cabin door.

Alone now. The rum throbs peacefully in his skull. He lies back. His mouth is dry and sour. His beard still smells of lavender.

His dreams land with exceptional force.

T
H
R
E
E

30.

Those on deck to hear their captain's speech are Obed Macy, Abner Cushing, William Lewis, Eben Tolling, Luis Buchard, Hiram Wiggins, Peace Rotch, Captain Upham, William Fish Williams, Henry Hays, Jeremiah Stone, Thomas Bird, Thomas Hobbs, William Thomas, T. Stubbs, Franklin Howland, Tomas Blevin, James Shoe, Tobe Eastman. The two boys, James and Tom Riggs. Below deck are also two pigs and five chickens, kept in pens near the galley, though they mind themselves as the captain speaks from the aft-deck to those gathered:

"Rules are to be obeyed," he says, "and must be. I make the rules on this ship. If you see a whale, sing at the top of your lungs. If you see a disturbance in the water you think *might* be a whale, sing at the top of your lungs. If I wish to speak to you, I will initiate the conversation. Otherwise, we are a quiet ship. If you are given an order by myself or one of the mates, you are expected to perform this duty to the best of your ability.

"If you neglect your duty, or disobey an order, you will be punished. You will hang you by your arms, and I will do the winching myself. I like a silent ship. I like a greasy ship. We will begin in the Azores and cruise Atlantic to Pacific, around the tail end of the world. We are heading to the Chukchi Sea. Any spotted fish will be taken along the way, but if we are light when we reach the ice, we will make up the difference with walrus. I am captain, and that is what I prefer to be called. We are not friendly, and I will not learn your names. I will call you men, and I will call you, *you,*" pointing, "boys. You are part of the *Esther,* now. You are her blood and bones. We should consider our directive a divine one and bless this work as it will better our stations. For the duration, you have no one above me to appeal. May this ocean reveal her giving self. May we take what she has hidden. Let's fill the hold."

"Eyes up," he calls, and the crew is dismissed to their duties.

The buildings of New Bedford slowly shrink to the *Esther*'s stern. Soon, they are indistinguishable from the rest of the tree-covered, blossoming land. In front of her, the sea stretches in every direction like a flat canvas strung to the apparent horizon, painted Prussian blue, glaucous, steel.

The sky is gray and undifferentiated.

The breeze picks up and dimples the top of the waves.

"Well done," whispers Thule. "I heard from my cabin." "Thank you," says Arnold Lovejoy. He taps his breast pocket, where he carries his present from Sarah Ashley. "It's an old speech. I've spoken it before."

"Just the same."

32.

"Do not fall!"

On deck, the boys have jumped to the *Esther*'s rigging and climbed to the top of the mast where the hoops sit. "Little ones!" the mate calls again. He waves to get their attention. "Do not fall from there!" he says, cupping his hands. "I've seen it."

But the boys can't hear him, for at their height the wind whistles low and deep into their ears and leaves room for no other sound.

In the hoops now, they brace with their hands, push and stand.

Ashore, when the signing agent heard of their circumstances—no mother, no father; no money; little food; one awful experience after another—he'd placed his hand on their shoulders. "It shudders my soul." He would've preferred to sign older boys on the manifest, but no one wanted to hunt the polar whale, and if you had no other names, you filled your line and looked to the next. "The ship will teach you," he said. He'd sent younger children to sea before. Many of them had taken sick or died. Pity. But no one ever came knocking on his door about it when they were orphans.

They are ten and twelve years old. He'd written their ages as twelve and fourteen. "Life's tragedy ends," he said and signed them in. "Shudders my soul."

They pull salt air into their lungs. The sun is close on their necks; their shirts snap behind them like flags in the wind.

Below, they can see the men scurrying about on deck, trimming sails, stowing gear, laughing. Neither boy has been farther from New Bedford than the Dartmouth Harbor, never farther into the blue water than a quick row. Within a few hours of departing, they see nothing at all of that old land. Goodbye, they call, farewell! We'll never see you again!

"Do not fall!" the mate cries once more. This time they hear but pay no mind. Of course they will not fall; they are determined to spot each whale the *Esther* darts. High above the deck now—they think of themselves as small birds gifted with quick flight. Or no, they are large birds. Frigates, with keen eyesight and sharp talons. In the rigging, they are monkeys in the jungle.

33.

The Ashleys, at the docks for the sendoff, had watched until the *Esther*'s masts were small on the horizon. They saw that her royals were set. She was of the ocean now, each sail plump with a pushing wind. "The path is long, but the *Esther* shan't fail," said Ashley to his wife and daughter. "Thule shan't fail. No, no. Lovejoy shan't fail."

Sarah Ashley said nothing. She was thinking of the captain, and the way he'd held her wrist.

With the ship out of sight, they stand near the water as the sun dims. "You've done your part," Ashley whispers. "Brilliantly," says Mrs. Ashley.

"But it will take years," says Sarah Ashley.

Ashley places his hand on hers. "It passes. Some live, some die, and some suffer at sea. But it is the ship herself who carries our appetite." As they turn from the harbor to make their way up the hill, he adds: "And who's to say suffering isn't the point?" At their dark, stately home, the curtains are drawn, the fire already lit. The frail child's mewling will keep them awake until the *Esther* returns.

Years, she thinks again.

But they can be patient when patience is called for.

F
O
U
R

34.

Heavenly days! Behold!

In the morning, the sun breaks up and over the water and reaches for the *Esther* in such a way that it seems to the boys as though they are heading right for it, into it even.

In this early passage, when the wind blows faint and wan, the men lower the whaleboats from their davits for practice. Now the boys wonder if it's a matter of will. With no land in sight, they call to the whales. *Rise*, they think, *rise*. For six days at the rail, they spot a few ships on their route, but no spouts.

The *Esther* in calm weather; the weather luffs her sails. In the evening, the sun sets, red, large, and salutary, over her stern.

And at night the sea feathers, nests, and stills.

The whalemen they have come to like are the old hands, sun-colored, with wild beards and roosters tattooed on their feet. The boys watch the easy way these sailors have with one another, their comfort on deck in the *Esther*'s pitch. This group works ahead of their orders and gives the mates no trouble. Topsides, they are quiet, bent and reverent to the task at hand. When not on duty, they tie Turk's head knots and sketch old ships to speed time.

To help the blacksmith at his grindstone near the main-mast and hatch, they hand him flensing knives and spades. They gather the toggle-headed darts from each steerer and return them when sharpened. The blacksmith has a back like a bear's but has been made a lop-side by the forge. He walks the deck in a herky-jerky way; it's as though time stops and accelerates for him alone. He will not be rushed. "Watch," he says. "Listen. Don't speak."

They do. They learn to sweep the deck shavings leeward, to pass a man on his right and not to his left. They learn never to speak when spotting unless at a whisper, to ask the mate's permission to come on deck. They learn never to address the captain directly, which they don't, as they haven't seen him much at all.

But there are rules they know, and rules they don't. One calm morning, the younger boy whistles as he coils line, and without explanation, the second mate rushes from under the midship shelter to slap him hard across the face. One evening they eat their supper before the whale-man's prayer and receive no food the following day.

In time, they notice only a few of the men do the bare minimum before retreating sullenly to the fo'c'sle. These are ones who have not been to sea before, Eastman, Fish Williams, and Stone—all three large and lumbering, surface-eyed and mean. In their limbs they carry casual violence. The boys learn to stay clear.

Eastman, in particular, seems interested in them; he watches as they help the smith, sometimes like an old owl, sometimes like a hawk. His skin is scarred and gray. If they see him coming, they go quiet. They notice the effect he has on the others—the men part when they see him, bow their heads slightly. Without saying a word, he has become the king of the fo'c'sle and gets the most space.

He is the largest man, it's just how it is, it is just so.

Now in the blue water, the Atlantic wind blows, and at full sail, the *Esther* is a golden bowl skipping over the sea. She feels, to all aboard, a fortunate bark; she has history in her planks and beams. But none will feel comfortable, or even fully settled until the first whale is spotted, struck, and stripped. "And what will you do?" the smith asks the younger boy. "Celebrate," he replies. The smith puts his finger to his lips. "Don't curse it."

Rise, they think, *rise!*

38.

To them, the sea appears like a curtain, pulled over.

But perhaps that is how it goes. A week passes, passed. The sun hangs over the *Esther*'s spars as though pinned to the sky. The men move this way and that on the deck. The dry light on the water forms a solid band across the leaden waves. *Rise*, they think. *Come to us!*

Each day ends without a single sighting.

39.

The weather is favorable, but they spot neither ship nor whale. "Patience," the smith says. Each day is the same. By now, the boys know the *Esther*'s steerage and hold and can sketch from memory her cabins and tiny, sprouting rooms.

They know the lapping sound of the calm sea on her hull, and its slap when in hazard. They carry toggle darts and flensing knifes, razor-sharp lances. For the bowhead in the ice, they've stocked bomb lances and a darting gun. For the walrus, a set of Sharps rifles, axes, and clubs.

Nights on deck, they tune their ears to the forehatch and listen to the way the men speak to each other. While working, the men are quiet, but below, in the fo'c'sle, they groan and gossip like maids in a knitting circle; they make a running conversation that flicks and flaps to the boys' hearing and lodges in their imagination. *Things are different now, and so much worse. How much worse?* They speak of wide gyres and towering waves, flightless birds, and visitors on deck. *How much worse? The man was skinned alive!* They whisper of merciless captains, time aboard an Ashley ship, captained by Ashley himself, a glut of whale cut through with their cow-catching prow. *How much worse? Abandoned at sea!* The men disparage every landlocked man and every landlocked trade. *Around his neck he wore a golden ring, it called the whales to him. We killed each one.* They speak of folklore and spirits and swear that it's true. *He'll take your hat if he pleases. He boards ships to sink them and nobody knows!* The boys hear of ships crushed by ice. The great tragedy of the *Dromo* and the women they've known. *But none as fair as Ashley herself.*

They learn that when drinking, the men tumble and fight below. They fondly place their elbows on one another and sleep tenderly in the same bunk to wake in each other's arms.

This closeness is something they see one night when looking for Turk's head knots the men have tied and forgotten. Their search brings them to the fo'c'sle late at night, and late in the fo'c'sle they see it.

Jealous, they say nothing. They pocket the knots and creep back to their own bunks near the steerage. The sea takes what she wants; she renders the unfit down. But they can see their voyage in front of them. The sea will be theirs. They are wary, determined. *Rise.*

The whale—she stands no chance at all.

40.

The boys are below when the first call is made.

In the steerage, it's clatter and bowl, complete pandemonium. They follow and join the men who've assembled at the rail. "Where?" "North, off bow!" They push through the tight scrum of the gathered hands. They squint into the distance, shade their eyes. They see nothing at all. "There!" The seaman who called it points directly into the sun.

A disturbance in the water—dimples and small splashes, a mile to port—there! They do see it, white on blue, a roiling surface! But they watch for a quarter-hour and see neither tail nor spout nor slick, black back. The excitement gives way to something darker; the mood curdles. "Idiot," the second mate says. He pulls his hat from his head and snaps it over his knee. "It's fish," he says as he goes below. "Flying fish."

They see the school cluster and hop in terror as one from the water. Their scales catch the sun and reflect it; their wings are like cooked panes of sugar. They buzz like bugs before dipping back to the sea to flash below the waves. Above them, a flock of cawing white gulls has gathered. "Watch," someone says. It's a difficult situation for the fish. Below the waves, larger fish dine on them with impunity. And above . . .

At once, the frightened fish jump again, and the fleet of diving white gulls pluck these miraculous small creatures directly out of the air. "Lucky birds," someone says. But nothing could be more disappointing.

The day comes to a close.

41.

"What fish?" the smith says.

They tell him again the story of the flying fish and the gulls, and the larger fish who must've been below the surface, but the smith grimaces and waves them off. "I can think of nothing that interests me less," he says. He speaks again his advice: Do not be seen and stay out of the way. To speak only when spoken to and mind their own business. "Fish!" he cries and shakes his head. They are chastened by his gruffness. They think highly of him and wish for his good opinion in return. When they sleep, he often follows them into dreams where they hear the rough drag of iron on stone.

Now in their pockets, they keep the Turk's heads they've stolen from the men—on deck, they roll and worry them when looking for whale. The leads and bights make a tight and beautiful knot. In the evening, in their bunks in the steerage, they try to make their own, "Not like that," the older boy says. He takes the line from his brother. "Try this." But he can't cinch the knot either.

One night, as they lay in their bunks, they hear their passenger stir and leave his cabin. They strain to hear his conversation with the captain through the captain's closed door. But it's short, and they can make nothing out. In the morning, they wake to the sound of the cook rummaging

around in the galley. "Don't spend your whole life moping around," he says. He is speaking fondly to his chickens and two penned pigs.

The day ends without a sighting.

42

When the Azores finally hump and peak on the horizon, all hands are called, and the archipelago is greeted like an old friend. These islands are famous: many ships have made their entire hold here. "There they are!" "The green island! The white!" The men crowd the rail and scan the water for any disturbance at all. "Eyes up!" Arnold Lovejoy emerges from his cabin expecting one thing but finds another: mountains that rise from the blue swell like giant's teeth.

They are jagged, green, more vertiginous and sharper than he remembers.

On reefed sails, the squinting men patrol the grounds all morning. But they see nothing. Nothing is turned up, nothing breaks. No vaporous spout, not one slapping tail. Not a single thing in the ocean.

Rise.

The *Esther* herself: she is the floating home to a crew of patient hunters. "Goodnight," Lovejoy calls. "Goodnight," answers the mate. He rings the bell twice, tolling the dark water.

"This is not my knife," says Eastman.

When the boys look at him quizzically, he pulls the youngest to him and quickly cuts the top button from the neck of his shirt. "Wrong one. Give this to someone else and bring me mine." They bow their heads and return below. They find the longest blade, sharpen it, and, when he makes no complaint, set it in front of him. To the youngest he tips its point. "Empty," he says, and they smell his rotten breath. He tips it then at his brother. "Empty." He tips it to the water, which glistens in the sun like strange, distant music. They've sailed slowly for twelve days and seen nothing.

"Empty, empty, empty."

44.

The waters aren't entirely empty, however, for on their last day in the Azores, the *Esther* is joined by a lone dolphin. As the men hoist the whaleship's royals, and those sails catch the wind, he noses around and keeps up playfully near the bow.

Underwater he moves like a blot of quickly spilled ink. Only when he breaks the surface does he reveal his full shape.

From the rail, the boys watch his dives—he is a fast and eager swimmer, concerned only with entertaining himself in the water. They look for others, but he has come to them alone, he has no pod, and to everyone aboard, he seems to be saying: the water's nice, perhaps join me. He reminds them of a wet dog. The men, with little else to do, decide to spear him for the sport of it. Up goes a mocking call.

One of the steerers grabs a dart and, at the sprit, takes up his throwing stance and holds it for all to admire. Those watching whistle and holler. The boys cheer too, but they are also thinking *dive*. "To hell you go!" "A straight shot!" "For rum!"

On three, the steerer tosses. He misses badly. "Good lord!" "Shameful!" Now, *this* is an unfortunate loss of face for someone in his position and will mark a tumble in the ship's esteem. The men jeer as the steerer complains that he rarely tosses from the deck—therefore, his angles are off; *therefore* it's not an accurate gauge of his ability. "Then do it again!" "Yes, once more!"

The dolphin remains on the bow, a good sport. *Try again,* he also seems to say, as he plays atop the waves with astonishing grace. The steerer retrieves his dart, lines up once more, and tosses—but this time knocks his foot on the ship's windlass, missing by an even wider margin.

The men find this delightful.

Unbothered by the attempt, the dolphin continues his arcing leaps, breaching in such regular intervals it seems as though, had he a needle, he might put a stitch in the sea. He looks, curiously, at the boys, with his black eyes unblinking. They return his gaze and feel blessed by it.

Then he dives, to be seen no more.

The men can't help themselves. To witness someone so starkly humiliated—it's the highlight of an uneventful day. "Again! Once more!" The cook is not pleased, however. "We'll never get home like that!" he shouts. He points to the sea where the dolphin had been, then wheels his fat finger to the steerer. "That's a *disgrace*. You're a disgrace. That fish gave you his belly!!" He spits over the rail. The steerer shakes with anger as the men disperse to their duties. The scene has served its purpose: a nice break, and now it's time to get back to work.

Alone now, the steerer retrieves his iron and coils its line. He stands in the bow's notch, a singular fool, and feels a hatred for the cook blossom like a dark coral. His heart grows very still.

He imagines cutting the cook's eyes out and tossing them into the sea.

45

"It is a beautiful night," says Thule. "It is the sort of night old sailors write letters about and remember when they are old."

It has been quiet in his cabin. Arnold Lovejoy puts down his pen. He listens to the night bells chime. There are no calls from deck. Mounted on the wall, near the ship's clock, is a single-flued dart, its iron old and twisted; it screws like a question mark. It had been pulled from a whale long ago.

On Ashley's chart, he's plotted the *Esther*'s course along the coordinates provided. Ashley has listed every whale struck by one of his ships: around the Azores the waters are smudged with small silhouettes. Yet as soon as they'd reached the islands, the sea had gone glass. It appeared lifeless, a reflective surface with no depth whatsoever, and they'd spotted nothing, neither spout nor breach, in their weeks under sail. "I never see you come in."

"That's because you are concentrating," Thule says, and lights another candle.

"Where are they?" "They are here." "Have they grown smarter? Are they gone?" "No." "I wonder now if Ashley's expeditions alone have put them on the verge of extinction, and perhaps we've made a mistake in coming here." "Have patience," says Thule. "We've only just begun."

Across the table, he glimpses Thule's flickering face. His hair is long, strandy, plastered to his skin. He remembers the last time he'd seen the Azores. He'd left his ship and walked the islands. He'd followed a hedgerow of blue hydrangeas to a hidden lagoon.

"I know of an old whaling captain who loved Ponta Delgada like a wife," Thule says. "To his son, he said: bury my heart there. His son, knowing how much the islands had meant to his family and fortune, assented. And when, later, the old man died, the son cut his heart out and stored it in a cask of rum until the ship made its return trip."

"Seven weeks in the wind and we've spotted nothing." Arnold Lovejoy moves his finger over the candle's flame. "I've been to Ponta Delgada. I was just a simple seaman then. My life still folded up."

"Your life is still folded up," says Thule.

From the mess of navigation equipment on the desk, Thule plucks the whaletooth Sarah Ashley had given Lovejoy and places it so the darting knot faces his companion. "And there is more to the ocean than the Azorean whale."

46.

When Thule has left, Arnold Lovejoy perches unhappily on the edge of his bed. *Blue hydrangeas*, he thinks. *A hidden lagoon.* He's eaten one of the small sweets that Thule brought him. It has become a habit, these nightly visits, and increasingly he's found that without them he is left too alone, to worry, to overthink. "For resilience," Thule had said. They are square and sodden and taste of dark sugar, from Ashley himself.

Sometimes, after eating one, he sleeps immediately. Sometimes not.

In the darkness next to him now sits his wife. She is young again, happy to see him. "It is as easy to grin as it is to growl," she says and laughs. She holds their twin daughters like sacks of small potatoes. He takes another drink. The memory candle snuffs out, reignites horrifically; she frowns and then she is gone. To calm himself he thinks of green water and sails on the horizon. He remembers returning to New Bedford years ago with a greasy ship, heavy in the water—his father's joy.

He closes his eyes. In time, he sees a passing ship crawl across the back of his lids; Sperm Whale, Right Whale, Bowhead, Humpback. With great relief he feels his arms go both weighted and weightless. "Eat," Thule had said. It does the trick. His lights go off, and he does not wake for hours.

47

As the *Esther* crosses the Atlantic line, Thule steps on deck. All movement topside stops. It's the first time the men have seen him, and in the midst of his sudden appearance no one knows what to do. He wears a long, black coat and a thick-billed hat; it casts a dark shadow over his thin features. The boys, from midship, cannot see his eyes.

Arnold Lovejoy, who had been speaking to the mate near the *Esther*'s aft-mast, steps forward and clears his throat. "This is Edmund Thule," he says. "He is our passenger and guest. And he has business on the ice."

"Gentlemen," Thule says, and removes his hat. "Do not mind me."

For an hour he stands unmoving in the middle of the deck, back straight, his hands clasped at his waist. With his mannered stiffness and long hair, he seems to the boys as though he's emerged from a different time altogether. "Bad luck." "Quiet." The men resume their work, but their eyes flick to him cautiously. Though they see he's staring intently at the water, no one can tell what he's looking at. Finally, he raises his arm to point. "There," he says softly.

It's not immediately clear what he's seen. He keeps his finger raised. The boys watch their captain come down from the aft-deck to stand at Thule's shoulder. They wait; then they understand. What he's seen is movement on the water, but what he draws their attention to is not a whale, but a large, black-faced frigate bird, gliding in the distance.

The bird is a graceful flyer; he stays close to the waves and rides the wind at his will. He is half a mile away. "Pretty bird," the mate says.

Thule lowers his arm and says nothing. He nods once to the men, gathers his coat behind him, and goes below. Minutes later, the boys watch as the captain follows. "So, he speaks to birds," one of the simple seamen says.

"Captain's business," the mate says. "Eyes up."

It's true, it is the captain's business, and the crew won't question it. They are an empty hold on an empty ocean; they know their jobs and their place. It isn't the strangest thing to have a gentleman aboard. "A surprise, that's all."

But to a man, they are relieved by Thule's departure.

F
I
V
E

48.

It happens one morning as the sun breaks over the port rail, all hands sleepy, that the large, black-headed bird returns. He circles her mainmast mast once, leaves her to scout the waves, then, with a tip of his wing, joins the *Esther* in her doldrums, gliding nearby not three feet above the surface of the water.

The men have seen no bird like this up close and, with little else to do, gather at the bow to watch his flight. His wingspan measures at least six feet. The feathers on his wings are the color of snow. A pure streak of white cast across a deep gray sky and sea. He burns himself into the mind's eye.

The *Esther* is miles from land. The bird floats in the soft air with the greatest of ease. And just when it seems as though a wave will reach him, he tips his tail and turns on a gust unfelt by those on deck. Then he rises. "He's back." Suddenly, to stern, the quiet sea parts—and up from the depths, with the water draped and splitting over his black, enormous, and rounded spine—up with an exhalation that sounds like a sharp, phlegmatic cough—up breaks their first whale. "Lower!" the mate cries.

It's as though the whale has called it himself.

The whaleboats, released from their creaky davits, splash to the *Esther*'s side as though in celebration. Each mate climbs into his favored boat, and the crew scrambles behind. The boys fetch their sharpened whalecraft and hand them down as instructed—*me, mine, that's mine, here.* "Pull!" The chase is on.

Though the whale is half a mile away, the boats close the distance in no time at all. "Pull!" Each man puts back to oar. "Port!" As they come close, he blows once more and the reaching air turns from salt to musk; a thickly exhaled haze-vapor, saturated with the interior smell of this great beast. But he is not a fast whale. His dives are shallow, half-hearted, thoughtless. He noses around and make small dips below the waves. Perhaps he is alone and has lost his way navigating this great ocean. It's possible he is looking for other creatures like himself. But he's found the *Esther*, or they've found him. Either way, the men will not let him go.

The second mate's boat reaches him first.

From twenty feet, the steerer makes his toss. The dart flexes and bows in the air, not a graceful throw, but a true one. The iron sinks into the whale's skin and holds. Surprised, the beast pricks and dives; the fast rope whistles on the chock and uncoils from its tub with thumping speed. The six seamen stow their oars and cling to their seats in preparation for the pull. The mate and steerer switch positions. The whale rises, exhales, and, in his terror and bewilderment, dives again. This time, he pulls the whaleboat behind him across the choppy water.

Finally, he tires and returns to the surface once more.

Now, the mate strikes with his lance—twice, a third time—and once fully in, plunges and churns the blade like a man furious with himself. He tugs and pushes, urges and nudges; tugs and pushes again. The men in the boat cheer him on. He can feel the resistance on the whale's interior, his flesh, sinew, artery, and the iron doing its cutting. A pop and the whale's blood blows dark. "Eyes up!" one of the men says in triumph.

And with one final exhalation, his blood vapor painting the bow of the waist boat, the whale expires.

He is a slow-swimming right whale.

Why he still swam in these waters after the almost wholesale slaughter of his genus is anyone's guess. Perhaps it is in his nature. Because he is so slow, and because he floats when struck and killed, and because he is found generally in the Atlantic, he almost single-handedly opened the American whaling industry. One doesn't even like to think about it. Among sailors he is known as the "gentle fish." He does not fight as hard as his brothers.

And though he swims much of the sea, he is such a deliberate and easy traveler that he carries an entire ecosystem on his insulated body: barnacles on his face, oysters on his rib-ends.

He's a skim-feeder, one of the ocean's great mowers, and in his mouth can be found two hundred and sixty-six pairs of sifting baleen, which, when chopped and extracted, measure between two and six meters each. His belly is white and milk-flashes when he sounds; his testicles weigh close to one ton; he renders to "brown oil." His baleen is used mostly for vanity: wasp waists and such. Sailors have reported a phenomenon with this particular fish: now and then, he will lift his tail out of the water and hold it perpendicular to the waves so that it catches the wind (a pose he can hold for twenty minutes or more). In this way, he is a bit of a sailor himself.

But this kinship buys him nothing.

The men pull the dart line aboard and recoil it. They sing. One seaman wonders how he will tell this to his sister when the voyage is over. *It had not been what I imagined,* he will begin. For the chase had been far slower and less exciting than he'd expected—he'd never had a doubt they would triumph and slay the fish. But he *did* smell his breath and see him part the waves like a loaf of black bread. Perhaps embellish the size of the catch, and the duration of the pull, perhaps drop the temperature a bit, add a shark or two . . .

The enormous whale floats dead, this wet and once-living island; he's no longer of the deep, nor will he swim the great sea again. Beautiful creature! For him, and for all hunted things, one might shed a tear—but it will make no difference.

The other two whaleboats catch up. A hole is cut directly into his flukes, a chain looped through and fixed. And then the exhausted, elated men begin to row their right whale by his tail the mile or so across the water to the waiting *Esther.*

50.

The boys had stayed perched atop the midship shelter, and from there had watched the scene unfold with excitement. As the whale was announced, they'd helped lower the boats and shouted encouragement as the men began their chase. But given the distance of the whale, and the sun's glare, they couldn't in fact see very much at all. Soon the whole enterprise felt decidedly less enthralling. From where they'd stood on the *Esther*, the men were indistinguishable in their boats—the scene all had the feel of an unfamiliar play watched from very far away.

For one thing, the whale did *not* loom in the way they'd expected. In fact, almost no part of the whale had even been visible to them from where they'd stood on the ship.

They *had* seen the water churn, and now and then glimpsed a white spray of the whale's desperate exhalations as they atomized and dispersed. They'd seen the boats row in their direct line as though tugged forward by the slowly fleeing beast. As for the melee itself, it appeared from their distance as though the mate in the forward boat was simply slapping the water with his lance. But then they'd seen the crimson death junk bubble from the whale's head; they'd seen the water go brown in a circle around the carcass.

And that had felt good.

51.

The steward, carpenter, blacksmith, and cooper ready the *Esther* for processing. They lower and secure the cutting platform, set the block on the yard and yardarm, sharpen long spades and knives, clear out the iron trypots. The ship is ready to receive her catch. But rowing a whale is a slow business, and a period of waiting begins. "Stay comfortable," calls the smith. "They'll be here soon." And it is during this lull a curious thing happens. The black-headed bird, whom they'd seen earlier and had all but forgotten during the hunt, glides back to them over the waves. With a long, arcing turn, he sets down heavily on the *Esther's* afterhouse.

It's such a surprise, and the bird so large, that all other movement aboard the whaling ship ceases. From a distance, perhaps to those rowing with their catch back home, it might have appeared as though all on deck were patiently awaiting orders from their feathered captain. The bird's eyes are dark and gemlike. He looks from one man to another. He slowly cocks his head.

Though the two shelters are separated by the mizzenmast, the boys are close enough to touch him. No one moves. Finally, the bird stretches his long neck and looks directly at the younger of the two. Neither knows what to say or do. Finally, the younger boy puts his hand to his heart.

The white-bodied bird bows his beak.

This quiet meeting does not last very long, however, for the blacksmith, well-known for his hatred of birds, jumps into action; he clangs and whisks two cutting knives together. "Begone!" The carpenter chimes in with a holler, and the spell is broken. Their visitor lifts his wide wings. Like a man hauling himself to dock from water, he seems, momentarily, to struggle mightily against his own weight. Then, with one massive, unfolding flap, he lifts, turns, and is suddenly free and gliding over the waves.

"That's a glutton," the cooper says. He clears his throat and spits over the gunwhale. "He came for your hat." "No, no," says the blacksmith. "He's white, not black." "His head," says the cooper, "his beak—a tubenose. Can't have him stay." The blacksmith sighs and shakes his head. It's not an argument that will be settled soon.

52

The unlucky whale is brought alongside the *Esther*, the cutting platform dropped to his back; the flensing men, wearing spiked shoes, board him like a rudderless vessel. He is sliced and hooked to the *Esther*'s block and tackle, and as each blubber-strip is hoisted, he turns in the water like a hog on a spit. With a tremendous sucking sound, each heavy piece is peeled and cut from his body and hauled onto deck. It's his black rind they are after.

His floppy, limp, and lifeless head is also severed and lifted, to be butchered on deck.

When the *Esther* holds what she needs from the whale, the second mate gives the order for the men to abandon the cutting platform. They do, and then the stripped and fleshy carcass is cut loose to sink, headless, under the waves. "Back to hell!" someone cries.

Thereafter, this enormous, wrecked mass drifts all the way to the ocean floor: bare and stripped of light, pulling to dark, a meal for the bottom-dwellers.

53.

On deck now, the head. One man brings an axe to the whale's jaw and splits it with a series of tremendous wet cracks. Then he and a friend go to work chipping out strips of feathery baleen. These, once cut, are stacked near the companionway like wet wood to be scraped and bundled later. Another man digs with a short knife for the weighty tongue—he tugs and cuts at the dark mouth muscle as though wrestling an alligator. Finally, it detaches.

Meanwhile, two other men have set about the problem of skinning and chopping his tall penis, which has also been hoisted aboard.

In life, the whale's head had been the size of a carriage. No more. It's disassembled, in pieces on the slick planks of the *Esther*. All that remains untouched on his once-great aspect are his useless eyes. In final salute, the men cut these out as well, for some think it lousy luck to be looked at in such a way.

54.

The heat generated by the tryworks at midship is infernal. The glistening blubber, chopped and hauled from below, is placed by tongs into the pots' open mouths. One
man stirs and with his skimmer pulls pieces of crunchy
skin to the surface; these he plucks from the radiant oil
while the men find the boys and push them to the foredeck. "Down the hatch!" "Open open!" "For tradition,
for luck!"

The boys, shoved forward, are struck dumb.

The pieces of skin, held toward them with tongs, hiss
and crack in the air. They look for the smith but don't
see him anywhere. They look for the cook. And when
they see Eastman, holding his knife, their legs weaken.
"Men soon!"

They are now part of something that will occur no matter their wish. The crackled skins are pressed to their
palms; they stink and burn, they are too hot to hold; the
boys shake their hands to distribute the heat. "Down the
hatch!" They put the bits in their mouths, but they are
scalding; the younger boy spits his out. One of the men
picks the piece from the deck and holds it aloft with tongs.
"You have to." "If you don't, we shan't get another!"

From behind, someone grabs them both. Hands on their
forehead, rough hands on their jaws, opening their mouths.

They kick, it does nothing; they go limp. The pieces are shoved forcefully into their mouths, their lips are held shut. It's like fire on the tongue and the backs of their throats. "There it goes, there it goes," Eastman says. He steps forward and punches the younger boy's nose so he chokes. "Swallow," he says, and takes his head in his hands like an orange.

"And how about more?" "One more!" "No!" "Open!"

By the time one of the mates breaks through, the offending men have dispersed. "Don't just stand there," he says to the boys. His face has settled into a grimace of disdain. "It's through. It didn't kill you."

He sends them below.

55.

They help the cooper organize his shooks and bands; they hold his gear with shaky hands as he assembles the barrels. "It's just a game," he says. "Happens."

"He's hurt," says the older boy. He wipes his own mouth with the back of his hand. "He'll live," says the cooper, and taps his band into place. When done, he sends them topside.

The planks are soaked in fat-chum and gore. The whale has slicked and covered the *Esther*'s decks completely. It will be the boys' job to clean her, though not theirs alone.

They bend and scrub on their hands and knees. Their lips are blistering. The smell of the butchery is sour, metallic, and it clamors their noses and lodges squarely at the back of their raw and burned throats. Their mouths feel peeled off. They set their jaws and spit their own red lines only when necessary. Each man is set to his task, cleaning, settling, organizing for the next call. None in their position would expect a cure for such an upset, for such a shock of pain, but one might hope for relief.

They finish.

The *Esther*, with her belly full, rocks peacefully. At night, after willing their own pain down to a quiet thrum, when finally they have been forgotten and tumble toward sleep, the boys glimpse a figure standing quietly in darkness against their closed door. His legs are vines. His eyes, two small flowers. In an outstretched hand he offers them two pieces of tarred twine. "For you," he says. "What is it?" they ask. But he will not say. They accept his offering. They eat and feel better. In the morning, they wake and see they've each pulled a patch from the *Esther*'s hull near their bunks. With her wood in their stomachs, they rise to face the day. No one pays them any mind.

The barrels, upended and stored in the blubber room, have been marked "WO" for whale oil.

The day ends without a single sighting.

57.

Now that they've rendered their first whale, seventeen barrels altogether, with plenty of room for more, the feeling on deck is that the voyage will come to good. The cheerful spotters return to their stations. They feel awash in the promise of the day. A threshold has been crossed.

The *Esther* sails like a regal queen over the waves.

"Try this," says Thule. The cabin is dark. It's just the two of them. Lovejoy has been staring at the whale tooth, at Sarah Ashley's face. He puts it away. "What is it?" "Tinned fish, from the north. From Ashley himself." Opened, the fish is rank. "It's a delicacy. For good luck. For a good day." He eats. "That's incredible." Thule grins. "Have more. It's a celebration."

The next day, another spout in the distance. This whale is even slower than their first; he's speared and caught with ease. At the first prick of the lance, he flurries in the water, furious. They give him room as he slaps the water with his flukes. Among Atlantic whalemen this is called "playing the drums," and he herks this percussion for a while, an angry and surprised song dearly in need of a melody. Then he turns fin out and dies. "He's ours!"

But before they can fix securely to him, he sinks.

58.

The *Esther* navigates south as quickly as the wind can carry her. The men gather to watch the waves—there is a rhythm to it: lift, drop, swell. The sun rises and sets. Standing at the rail or within one of the *Esther*'s superstructures, the wide ocean holds the appearance of hammered tin. In the distance, the water is still and monochrome, as though a large painting has been hung around the ship, a work whose colors have been brushed by a skillful painter in order to direct one's gaze elsewhere. Day after day. Now the sea brings forth nothing; for weeks, it appears almost wholly unoccupied.

But the mood has calmed and the clocks are set. One rides the visible swell, and the *Esther* moves in tandem with the sea's exhalation.

The boys keep to themselves. They clean and scrub and do what's asked of them. They visit the pigs in the galley, feed the chickens in their pen. From the rigging they call the *Esther*'s beam and line, her crooks and coils. If the men are bored or made anxious by this lull in their voyage, they are not, for the cooped oil, their first, cannot be taken from them—it's safe, and barreled, below—and it feels as though they've been plucked from their orphan's life in New Bedford by God's own hand, on His reason and recommendation alone.

If they listen now, they can hear the sea calling to them—the plunge and wash of the water, its promise. They bury the memory of the men's hands on their lips and bodies. It's how men behave; the whale made them crazy; they feel part of the crew and it bothers them no more. Their mouths heal. They've chopped, barreled, and made use of the whale, his brown oil is currency. They've been placed in a corked bottle and sent somewhere new. The days pass without distinction. The countdown to the end of the voyage has begun in earnest.

Farther south, the sun, closer now, bands the dark water with sharp, glittering light. Soon the heat grows oppressive. The deck, hissing, dries by the afternoon. The warm wind is fluky. Some days she blows strong and from the north. Other days her gusts are sporadic and even limp— those come from the east and cause the sea to chop irregularly. The men are perplexed. But they are used to long stretches between sightings and the strange gifts of weather at sea.

When not at their tasks they sing. *He who swims / is he who strikes* . . . They tar line. Sew and set sails. They stay on deck, for in the heat the fo'c'sle has become a wretched place.

There is no cure for weather of this sort, and during this passage, the *Esther* feels in a heavy mood. But there is nothing to be done. One simply kicks through it.

They are near the coast of Brazil when the wind picks up and the otherwise blue sky suddenly goes dark. A sudden, and very loud, *crack*—it's as though the heavens have split or, inland, some large volcano has erupted. In a flash, the previously open sky fills almost entirely with thick, low clouds.

Ghastly weather. To the men's surprise, the sky, which until this moment had been bright and recognizable, plumes; and quickly they see birthed a succession of contoured and expanding clouds. At first, these clouds take the billowed shape of white columns that link sea to heaven. Then the wind picks up, and gusts begin to cut and pull these columns apart like straws drawn through foam. Across this agitated canvas the men now see the shapes of other ships. They see animals: a terrapin swimming through a jellyfish; a crab with open claws. Then, as though lined up in a chorus, they see their own expectant faces.

One more loud *crack* brings them back to their senses. Whatever the boys have seen, they won't say, but it leaves them quivering and close to tears. A third crack draws the men's attention heavenward where the clouds, now dark, have lowered to cover the sky. Then commences a lashing rain.

The swell increases, steeply; the rain drills and drums the deck. The *Esther* slaps and skids on her beam. For the first time, the boys are seasick. The cook helps them as he holds his own belly. Below, the shadows from the galley lamp dance in no pattern across the cabin walls—it would make anyone ill. They roll for a long day, then some unseen object diminishes the wind's fetch, and the ship stabilizes.

"Sweet relief." The cook wipes his brow.

61.

Soon after, Thule leaves his cabin and comes topsides once more. He climbs the rigging and crouches in the crow's nest; he mutters to himself in a way no one can decipher. He's been on a ship before—the men see it in the way he moves, which is confident, and sharp. Efficient. He makes no effort to speak to anyone. He returns below at four in the morning.

For five nights, he repeats this behavior, emerging in the evening to pace the deck with his hands clasped behind him like a moody friar. The seamen on deck don't fear him, yet his presence makes them uneasy. They begin to speak of him as though he exists only to spy on them and the work they do. *Return to your cabin and stay there,* the men complain as they pass quietly on deck. For five nights he sets them on edge. On the sixth, he does not leave his cabin, and the men catch no sight of him. They are relieved. He is unusual. His presence, his pacing.

In his absence, however, the wind drops completely, not even a whisper is felt. It cannot seem to raise itself day or night, and the *Esther* mopes about in her first depression.

62.

"What's happening?" the younger boy asks. "I don't know," his brother replies. At night, the sea looks dark and strange—obsidian, solid. During the day, across the calm water, which, unkissed by breeze, is mirrorlike, they can see South American land. This sudden calm brings with it a deep silence.

The men stop speaking. To contemplate the ocean's stillness in the night hours is to tilt toward something dark and depthless, abyssal. In daylight, it appears as though the sea is a thick, smeared lid—a reflective tray that hints at a solid layer below the surface.

Caught in irons of this sort, one is compelled to look inward. Best not to; best don't; it's enough to drive a man crazy. But after three days, the wind picks up and so does the current, and those aboard are rescued from the need to think any further on what they've seen.

63.

"Watch this," the older boy says to his brother.

During their lull, he's figured out how to tie the Turk's head knot. "It's just over here, then under. Then over again . . ." They are on the foredeck, with the merciful wind carrying them south once again. Through the hatch, they hear the men talk. They are arguing, but about what they can't tell. *It's not just this ship, everywhere is series of tragedies. Not just one. All ships now. Have you seen anyone else walk like that? A whale strikes and sinks a boat. It's miserable, there is not enough work, the voyage ends only in disorder. Where is the captain? Why is he so rarely on deck? Every ship has its problems. That was only one ship. Our wind dropped, but we are not stuck. It means nothing at all. There is nothing strange in it, nothing more to it. He's simply a passenger. There will be no tragedy here.* Their voices lift through the fo'c'sle companionway and in fragments catch in the boys' ears. After the long days of silence, they are relieved at the sound.

The foc's'le is dark and crowded. At night, rats burrow in the men's blankets and cockroaches nibble skin from their sunburnt lips. But once they fall asleep, nothing can wake them. *A blessing,* one might say of such deep slumber. At the very least, it is necessary.

64.

Only two notable events occur during this leg of the voyage. The first happens early one morning, in view of Cape Horn, when one of the simple seamen falls to his death from the uppermost yard. Perhaps the dawn caught in his eye, or perhaps his mind had wandered—it hardly matters. He feels the shove of gravity, yelps, snags once on the rigging, and plunges straight down.

He'd been unfurling the main gallant topsail, something he'd done many times before. He'd been an able sailor, and yet! He hits the *Esther*'s planks with a slap as loud as a shot from a small cannon.

From anywhere on deck, one can see his neck is badly broken. The boys are the first to his collapsed side. Half his face is caved in. "Cook!" they cry. "Cook!" They look away. There's nothing to be done. The man gives two rasping, begging breaths there on the deck; blood drains from a hole near his ear and pools under his head. The cook cups the man's tremoring hand as though it's a shivering bird. He expires.

65

"Help me," the cook speaks to the boys. They take hold of the seaman's legs and move his body to the galley. His head leaks and drips down the steps as they bring him below. They've never seen a dead man before. He is to be washed and lain out, then sewn into canvas with weights at his feet. At sundown, he will be given a proper burial. On the galley floor, now, the cook drapes a cloth over the man's face. He kneels and begins unbuttoning the man's shirt. "He feels nothing," the cook says. "Don't be shy."

They begin by unlacing his shoes. They remove his socks. His toenails are caked, dirty. His feet are still warm. The cook is quiet. Once stripped of his clothing, the man is scrubbed with a dish brush. The boys go topside, return with a bucket of water. With rags, they carefully squeeze the salt sea over the man's chest, hips, groin, legs; he moves not at all. They are overcome with the urge to touch his ruined face but do not. When they are finished, the cook takes the bucket, removes the cloth from the poor man's blank visage, and sluices the blood from his hair until he's clean. "Mark your name," he says, and hands each a small piece of sailcloth.

The men line up on the companionway, silent. Each approaches the dead sailor and kneels; each grimly, delicately, place a snatch of cloth with their own names into his open mouth. "It's for Old Sorrel. It confuses him," the cook explains. The boys do as they're told—they fold their cloth and place it behind the dead man's broken teeth, push down on his cold tongue; they nestle their names with the others. The men stand near and watch. "A secret," the cook says, by which he means not to tell the captain. Then he bends over the poor man's face and, with a needle and thread, begins to sew his blue lips shut.

A final tug, a darting knot; the cook reaches now to close the poor man's eyes. They have been open and empty the whole time, watching them. "Boys, out," he says. They're ushered to the steerage and the door to the galley is closed.

The men gather aft of the mast as the sun goes down. Passages from the book are read aloud by the first mate, and finally their captain emerges from below to cross himself. They say nothing as the dead man, sewn completely in canvas, is briefly remembered and, with no further overture, tipped overside. He slips below the waves, into a nameless part of the sea.

"Shame."
  "Shame."
  "It's the life."
  It is.

"Eastman has one of the dead man's fingers," the younger boy whispers to his brother. "What?" the older boy says. "Where?" But he doesn't need to look hard, for the goliath Eastman, in the morning light, sits near the foc's'le hatch, cross-legged, eyes closed, the finger on its side like the blunt end of rope in front of him. None of the men say anything. They give him space. But the boys, horrified, and remembering what he'd done to them, pull the steward aside, and quietly tell him.

"See for yourself."

He does, and for this inhuman behavior the steward summons the captain, and soon Eastman is hauled to the afterdeck. It's clear he'll be punished. The mates hold him by his elbows. He looks twice their size. "Why have you done this?" the captain says. "I have no reason," Eastman replies. The steward plucks the dead man's finger from the deck and with a grimace chucks it into the sea.

The first mate brings the *Esther* close on the wind.

Eastman, tied to the mizzenmast, makes no sound during his punishment. He's whipped, and whipped again. "There is order," the captain says. "There is law. Natural law." Eastman says nothing. The boys watch from a distance. Finally, he passes out.

67.

The cook sets up a cot for recovery in the galley. Eastman is laid on his stomach. Upon inspection, Arnold Lovejoy is relieved to find that most of the cuts are superficial—a proper cross-hatching, with only a few of ruptures requiring thread. His breathing is slow and measured. "How did this happen?" he asks the cook. "Did he unstitch the shroud?" The cook shakes his head. Carefully, Arnold Lovejoy pinches each abrasion shut and rinses Eastman's back with fresh water, for in addition to being the *Esther*'s captain, he is also her surgeon. Where there is cotton from Eastman's shirt pressed into the wounds, he fishes it out to prevent infection.

The sailor Eastman sits near the pinrail in the morning sun, flat light, whittling a small stick, recovering. The boys walk quickly past. Even hunched over he is large, and bulky; his skin, its peculiar shade of gray. His shirt sticks to his back.

Seeing them, he drops his knife. He doesn't reach for it. A vein over his eye expands, and the color returns to his face. He is the last man the signing agent had hurriedly placed aboard the *Esther*. "Was it you?" The boys say nothing. "Was it?" One of the mates tells him to quiet.

"Eyes up!" Eastman shouts, but doesn't move. "Eyes up, eyes up!"

For laziness and insolence he ought to be hung by his arms for eight bells, but as he is injured, he's allowed his perch for the day.

"Eyes up!" he shouts, breathes deeply, and speaks no more.

The boys climb the mast and settle. From the hoops they can see five miles in every direction. They look for the fallen man—*dead man*—but he's sunk clear to the bottom of the ocean, missing finger and all. The *Esther* dips and dodges with the swell. To port there is another whaling ship, heading home; she is a cream smudge of color near the horizon. They can feel Eastman watching them. They wish they'd said nothing.

The breeze comes in like a sharp song.

The men accept Eastman's punishment as they would for any crewmember. What the captain wishes is done, his desire is the ship's, and is theirs as well. It was unusual, but it's over now. At the proper time, Eastman will return to his duties and the ship will regain composure. A dead man; a severed finger; a beating; then equilibrium found in the task at hand. The boys would like to imagine Eastman punished for what he did after they caught their whale, but they know it's not so. This is life at sea. They spit loudly into the wind.

Below, the men set about their work, washing the deck, straightening lines. Some stand at the rail like stone statues and watch the creasing sea.

There is not a cloud in the sky.

70.

Something about all of this amuses Thule greatly. "What is the standing of God on this ship?" he asks. Arnold Lovejoy sighs and folds his hat. "I am God on this ship," he says. "That's the right answer." Thule taps his front teeth with one of his fingernails. "You shouldn't feel *guilty.*"

Arnold Lovejoy stands. "You've missed the point."

Thule smiles. In the low light, his sharp and long features look as though they'd been sketched in charcoal. But his eyes are bright. They glisten and flash like peeled grapes. "Ashley would've killed him," he says.

S
I
X

7*1*.

"Each day without a whale is wasted time, a day that does not happen." "It's well-known." "But we must get to the Pacific before we can expect to lower again." At this, Thule nods. "Do we go high or low?" Lovejoy says. But Thule is no longer in his cabin, and as the *Esther* begins her attempt around Cape Horn, a quiet grace is recited in the fo'c'sle: *clement, clement, clement.* The weather is unusually agreeable, the swell tall and consistent; they clear the decks and navigate on cleated sails. Their first day is seamless. But the good weather they've enjoyed cannot hold forever, and does not.

On their third morning of the crossing, the sun rises red and pink, almost twice its normal size. The men stop what they're doing to watch as it hushes and climbs. They know what it means. Soon, the wind comes up and begins to sing. The low light turns green near the horizon.

Rain falls in strings from the sky.

72.

The *Esther* bears the rising waves as she's built to. Her bow slices and plunges; spray flumes over her sprit, hangs momentarily in the air as though espaliered, then drops. The men curse and hold their stomachs, heavy one moment and weightless the next. Everything not secured smacks below deck. Most of the cutting instruments come loose from their bindings and clatter like pots and pans with each pitch. "Hold tight." "Hold!"

The sudden darkness from the low clouds turns the steerage into a shadowland. The troughs between the waves move like slinking canyons. Topside is no better. The rain sounds a slapping cannonade on the *Esther*'s wet wood and turns her deck to a slick tray. Each pitch sends her to her rail, and with each wave over her bow it seems as though the ship is working to push through the swell rather than ride it. Fight, fight! The *Esther* heels like a toy ship; every drop into the troughs concusses her hull. The howling wind plays over the white-capping waves, which surge forth as though in a charging brigade. Each wave then folds and rolls as though avalanching down the steep face of a mountain.

Neither of the cook's two pigs, poor fellows, could have imagined this. One, frozen in fear, huddles in a happier spot, perhaps in deep contemplation; the other scrambles in his pen and finally breaks out. As he slips and clatters around the tilting ship, he squeals as though stuck through—and it's his screeching, rather than the waves themselves, which confirms for the men huddling below that their days are numbered. "It's the dead man's revenge!" "Catch that pig!" But to what end? There's no point in numbering days. There is nothing to be done now, everyone knows that. This is the cape crossing. Most have done it before and lived. The weather is a fact, a chapter in a story that must be read aloud to every sailor and won't be rushed.

The storm, monstrous, roars and screams at the *Esther*. It tears at her sails and whips her rigging. It will last until it's over—it's simple as that. One can only trim his ears to keep the sound away. Or else let the sound obliterate upward feeling altogether. How long can one last otherwise? One day? Two days? The body is durable. Best not to think on it. One lucky seaman, washed overboard, finds himself placed directly back on the ship by the crashing waves themselves. He goes below and will not be moved.

From the deck, where he's lashed himself near the wheel, Arnold Lovejoy occasionally sees the sun break through the rolling black clouds in the distance like golden-beamed fingers. *Help me*, he thinks. Now and then one of these fingers illuminates the deck in what looks to be a sturdy column of misted light. But these touches are fleeting. They are nothing to hold onto. One simply imagines better weather, elsewhere.

He cannot remember seeing worse water.

In such hazard, seamen think only of before and after. A day, a week, who knows? Time isn't the issue; and though it passes, it does not obtain. One enters this canal innocent and emerges crying and silty. But then it really *is* over. The wind drops as quickly as it stirred up. The clouds part. It feels to all as though large, unseen hands have pushed the *Esther* through a heavy curtain and dropped her on a separate side of the stage. Relief. The men gingerly hoist themselves topside. Here is the sun, now.

Their bodies are sore. They have no voice in their throats.

74.

Steam rises from the *Esther*'s deck as she shakes herself from the weather to face the new morning. In the distance, white clouds convect into glorious shapes off the bow—branches of living coral, French meringues—to greet them. As the boys climb the mast, the damp rigging squeaks at their weight. From their perch, they can see the *Esther* has been well washed. She looks new.

And to stern, they can see their old storm sweeping darkly behind them, prowling and punishing the sea.

75.

After an inventory, it's determined the only casualty of the crossing has been the cook's unlucky, scampering pig. He's found tucked under a pot, eyes closed, his full face finally at rest. "From fright," says the cook. "Fright!" It's his belief that no one ought to cut up and serve an unslaughtered pig, and this one, lost at sea . . .

He carries his dead friend topside. There is no ceremony, but most of the men are there taking in the sun, grateful themselves to be alive. They are appropriately solemn. The cook says a few words to the pig that no one can hear. Then, with the help of the steward, he rolls the great, limp swine over the side. He drops with a fat splash and sinks.

His troubles are over.

"You seem surprised that she is so well-built," says Thule. It's true. The *Esther* is fine. She's lost neither men nor barrels and is virtually unmarked. "We were lucky," replies Arnold Lovejoy. "No," says Thule. "It was not luck."

During the worst of the storm, an image had come to Lovejoy, one he will not share, of Sarah Ashley settled on the spars. She looked toward him, lashed to the *Esther*'s wheel; she bowed her head. It was as though she'd been placed there to see them through. She wore white, and her feet were fixed to the same spot from where the poor seaman had fallen not two weeks ago. He'd called out to her. She disappeared.

He's found it, and holds it now: the whaletooth. He can feel its heat in his hands.

He is just happy to be alive.

"I, myself, felt no fear," says Thule. "We could not have been safer. You've walked the *Esther* in admiration, have you not? Her stern piece, near where you are sitting, is cut from live oak. Her knees are hemlock. You've noticed the oddities in her construction. Her history is indescribable. Thousands of whales have slicked and washed her deck. She's gone icebound in the Beaufort Sea—a full season in the pack-ice as her starving crew clung to her rails. The pressure on her hull would've crushed lesser ships, but she bore it. She's chased the right whale into typhoons, and she bore it. The sea has been after her for years. Yet, she will not buckle, she will not break, and she will not be dissuaded from doing what she was built to do.

"Nor will we. In my travels I have seen weather that would leave you breathless. Nevertheless. How should I put this so you will understand? On the coast of Jamaica there exists a red hermit crab. Exquisite creatures, nearly impregnable, perfect in design. But one must remember that their famous shells are not their own. Without some other creature's former home as protection, these little bugs are helpless. Their tails curl like grubs, they are limp, vulnerable, even their claws have little pinch. They are so soft and unformed that they will die in the sun. As they grow, they shed one shell and move to the next. And one would think that these old shells, now abandoned, are no longer of use to the crab. But consider this: it may be that it is the crab who is no longer of use to the shell.

The *Esther* and her sisters, the fleet—they are such shells. You have wiggled your soft abdomen into these comfortable quarters, and you are the one setting her sails and charting her course, and she will protect you, have no doubt. But in your heart, you know that it is the ship that chooses her captain, and while you and I may come and go, the *Esther* will outlast the two of us. She will always take to the water. She will turn it the color she wants. She will deliver us to the ice, and to Leander. And after that, what you do will be up to you. She's been doing this for a hundred years. A little storm was not going to frighten her."

78.

"And what of the *Dromo*, Leander's ship?"

"That is a different story, altogether. It is one, perhaps, he will tell when we see him. I am as curious as you are. We are halfway, now. We will not turn back. What awaits us is our reward. There is no point in thinking too much on it. We move forward. We will endure. We will claim what is ours. We always have."

"You can tell me what you want. What do you desire?"

Lashed to the wheel, and afraid for his life, Arnold Lovejoy had seen the delicate skin of a lavender-scented wrist. A wasp waist. Half-covered, flushing breasts. *I could explain everything to you*, she'd spoken from the spars. *It would be wrong to do so.* In the calm water now, he feels shame and exhilaration. He knows what he wants. *My hand on yours . . . I have come through and the storm is behind me . . . Wait . . .* He's already writing a letter in his head.

He will say nothing of this to Thule.

"I want more fish."

"That's right." Thule smiles, then is gone.

The storm is still in the boys' ears; it's not a sound they can shake. Their limbs are battered, the steerage in disarray. Warm night. Long night. That they've survived seems a miracle.

"If you could be anywhere, where would you be?" "I would be right here, on the waves." "Steering the ship?" "I'd be the captain, and I'd steer the ship."

"You'd find the whale?" "I'd call them to me." "And all of the fish?" "I would call them to me." "And all of God's creatures?" "I'd call them to me."

The bells chime, and the men off watch tumble below.

"Poor pig," the younger boy finally says.

"Yes," his brother agrees. "Poor pig."

S
E
V
E
N

80.

Near the Galapagos, they see terrapin, jellyfish, and crane. The islands rise from the water like a knuckled spine. The boys spot finches, fur seals, doves. A colony of sea lizards like bald, ugly monks watch the *Esther* pass through. Further north, the men spear a sea lion from the rail, then a dolphin; then a second dolphin as sailfish hook over the distant waves. These are brought on deck and slaughtered, the sea lion's whiskers plucked, bunched, and tied, hung on the foremast for luck. As they near the equator, the sun grows restless; it bears down. On watch, the heat knocks inside the men's heads. Below, they sleep and fever.

One morning, they sail across a large, gelatinous mass. It floats near the surface, moving with the current, and lists under the waves like a sodden mainsail: a dark red stain on the sea. In the heat, it blooms like a strange flower—its stench is overpowering. Death, putrid rot; it's all one can smell. As the men look closer, they see tentacles, a massive eye, an open beak.

The wind pushes from the south.

They see no whale.

On they sail.

81.

To die of fright, and to not even be of use, plunked into the sea . . . it was the pig's fate and it has stuck with the boys. They remember his cries of fear in the storm, and it clenches their hearts. Perhaps it's because he could neither speak nor understand what was happening. He had been tossed about in near darkness without knowing to what end. The man they tipped overside with their names in his mouth—he has settled on the bottom of the sea behind them, and they don't think of him at all. But the pig is stubborn. He'd been so far from land, he hadn't belonged on board in the first place. He'd wandered about the ship like a big, rooting potato. "He must've felt great pain when his heart went."

A whaleship's cruelty is unavoidable. The whale is unsuspecting and, on the whole, gentle; there is no other way to see *that* part of it. But though the hunt itself is not kind, the speared fish are soon dead, and the utility of their bodies is a form of grace. "That's how to think of it." "It's how I will." And yet they wonder: After the pain of death, when he finds himself flayed, with their hands pulling and cutting his carcass, reduced to so much meat and meat only . . . Does he not feel pain then, of a different sort? Still warm, his blood washing the deck and pooling the waves? They can think of no better way to do what had to be done, but when the whale is brought close, and they touch and work with all their might to dismantle him, what is it they are pulling apart? And is he aware of himself? And embarrassed or ashamed to be so used? The men speak of cows lanced so that air gushes from their punctured lungs in torrents, bowhead drowning in their own blood. A bull with ten irons in his side, who surfaces in great suffering like an avenging vision from the deep. They go on and on; the boys listen. The men discuss one strategy in particular and speak reverently of its ruthless logic. Having spotted a pod, one must first aim to kill the calf. Its mother might dive out of fear, but since she will not abandon her child, and no matter her own fright, she will not sound long. She will return, and in grief may then be struck as well.

This lodges in their imagination. Perhaps it is because they are doing so little killing themselves.

The men are bored. With nothing to do, they watch the empty waves and begin to silo, estranged from one another, each man to his own thoughts.

One day, two days, three days, four.

82.

No one wishes to speak of what happens next, but it can't be delayed any longer. Almost as soon as the Sandwich Islands are in sight, the seaman Eastman, his large back healed and his heart black in a way that cannot be accounted for, follows the boys into the darkened steerage, closes the hatch door, and locks it.

He's been patient. And he thinks about it like this: a part of me that had been slumbering is now awake.

"Make no sound."

He's trapped them. And they see that in one hand he holds his penis; in the other, a glinting knife.

It's soon over.

They wish not to speak of it. Like the pig, they have no capacity to calm their own hearts. But someone must do something.

83.

In the morning, the sun pushes her light into every part of the *Esther* to wake the ship. She sees the boys. She places her fingers on the back of their bare necks and roots in their greasy hair. She sees the small spots on their backs, what Eastman has done and how it will change them. She sees them wash their mouths with salt water once he's left them alone, scrub between their legs and sit quietly in their cabin, sees the younger bruised and the older unable to comfort his brother.

But she can only watch.

They climb the companionway and walk shakily onto the deck and into the light of the rising sun. "Where've you been?" says the smith. He gives them each an iron dart and points to his grindstone.

84.

At midday, the steward's hat blows overboard. It catches the wind like a kite, dances a small circle off the port rail, and sinks. The men, upset, lower to retrieve it, but it's gone—the ocean has swallowed it. Bad, bad luck. The sun, warm now, sees this, too. It is she who has brought forth the breeze. But there is nothing more she can do for the crew of the *Esther*, what's done is done. She travels on her wheel. She offers no comfort whatsoever. The day is long. And when the day is over, and the boys, more careful now, barely themselves, leave deck for the evening, she lights up the moon.

85.

Alone in their cabin, the younger boy weeps. "Pretend none of this happened," the older boy finally says. "Pretend you are somewhere else." He leans over and wipes his brother's tears. "Now pretend," he finally says, "you are something else."

"It works. I promise."

They imagine a different ship, in a different part of the world. "I'm the captain, you're the mate." "No, we are both captains." "We're never going home." Off the bow, whales fluke and dive. "Dive!" They imagine giving what Eastman's done to them to someone else. They place it at the bottom of the ocean; a whale swims with it; it's with the broken-necked man. They dive down and greet him, sew their memories into his mouth. They weight him with this story so a new one might hold.

It works; the pain subsides. Now, in their bunks, they can be quiet. They have nowhere to go. There is no then, only now, and what comes next. They close their eyes. Don't speak of it. Don't think of it. Move.

Two nights later, the cook's pig returns to them in dream—cast in shadow, sitting near the dark edge of their bunks like the man who brought them twine to eat. When they wake, he is still there, quietly rooting around until the sun cuts through his presence and wipes him clean. For the next three nights, he visits in the dark.

They expect, in his company, they will feel better;

they look forward to it. On his fourth visit, he sits on his haunches, happy; aggressively, he gnaws on a bone of some sort which he holds between his two hooves. His expression is placid, calm. Perhaps, they think, he will remain a companion, only theirs. But on his fifth visit, something is different: the pig is discolored, and agitated. And as they watch, a large shipworm bursts from one of his ears—it's black, wet, sickly; it circles his gray, water-logged head, and wetly burrows deeply in the other.

They are horrified—

Yet the pig makes no sound. He endures the worm, and continues gnawing, working his bone.

When they wake, he is gone, and they know he's gone for good.

86.

As they approach the Sandwich Islands, the green jungle appears impenetrable, closed, lush and full, from the rail. The loulu palms bow and rustle in the heavy wind; their fronds are like thick hair reaching for the sky. The boys are in the hoops; Eastman is nowhere to be seen.

"We've been burning for weeks," says the depot agent. "Locals are restless." Arnold Lovejoy nods and looks around. Many of the buildings *have* been burned. "It's about sugar," says the agent. He, Lovejoy, signs for supplies and, with a slight tremble, takes a letter from his jacket pocket. "Has any mail come for me?" The agent shakes his head. "Of course. I'm not sure what I was thinking."

The letter is addressed to Sarah Ashley. It's a statement of sorts; he's written it in a fever. It's not fit to be read, but it's been sealed and now, almost against his will, he is letting it travel. He can think only of her.

"Can you put this on the next New Bedford–bound ship? It notes our progress." The agent receives his letter and marks it in his leger. "The Ashleys," he says, impressed. "Of course."

87.

He knows it's a young man's ailment. That he finds his own language inadequate, flowery and filthy, doesn't matter nor has it stopped him from writing. Since the storm, he's seen her face etched in nearly every part of the ship. Of the gift he's to present to Leander, he's begun to feel it is his, intended for him, inscribed for him alone.

She is with him now. When he dreams, she is his wife and his daughters, waiting. He remembers his own mother; his mother has her face. He thinks himself capable of doing nearly anything in her presence. He's *already* done these things in his mind.

It takes until the *Esther* has dropped her lines and is safely out of the harbor for Arnold Lovejoy to feel the first shudders of regret. But it's behind him, now. "North-bound we go," says Thule. "Indeed," replies Lovejoy. "Indeed, indeed." He can no longer sleep without Thule at his side. "Indeed, indeed."

EIGHT

88.

The sea flattens and lightens in color as they head north, and it is as though, having put the islands to stern, the whaleship has crossed some invisible meridian. They know these waters. The sun feels close, and when the men, even when not on spotting duty, are at the rail, they are anxious and expectant. The wind blows strange. It's in fluke—from the north in the morning, the south in the afternoon. But sure enough and soon, they receive their tropical welcome: a black whale in the distance. She makes one tremendous, arcing leap.

Up comes the call.

89.

The second mate holds his hat in his hand and slaps it like a tambourine. Another breach as they scramble. "Lower!" "She's big!" She is—and she jumps again. With each land-ing, the sea flumes around her.

In her graceful play, she seems to eclipse the sun.

90.

The *Esther* is fully alive now and her sound carries to the whale: the men's eager shouts, the careless clatter, the lowering of the boats—she hears them.

No fool, she turns tail and swims far and fast from the whaleship—but soon, perhaps from exhaustion or because she's forgotten their purpose, her swimming becomes less urgent.

Perhaps she is simply not afraid. No, no, the men see—she is just hungry. A mile into the chase, she finds a blanket of krill and opens her wide mouth. This slows her considerably; the boats catch up. She fills her gullet once more, turns widely in the krill cloud, and raises a fin as though in greeting; then she rights and swims slowly north, as though care never crossed her skull. It is here, digesting her last meal with the heat of the afternoon on her rough back, that she is struck—darted and held fast.

Now she swims, and dives with her burden, tugging the attached boat over the water. It's only a matter of time until she grows tired, that's just how it goes, but the question of how much time is firm in their minds. They toss a second dart, and a second boat attaches; this makes no difference. She pulls for hours. She takes no turns; she swims in a straight line and soon the *Esther* is well out of sight. Finally, she dives once more in confusion, tangled in the trailing lines.

Then she surfaces, exhausted, and is slaughtered.

The men, tired, embrace and place their hands on the dark skin of their catch. The *Esther* is miles away, but in which direction is anyone's guess. The horizon is flat and empty; they are alone on the sea, and the tug back, even if their heading is true, will take them into the evening. "It's her revenge." The steerer pats the whale's side with his lance. The men lie back in their boats or rest over their oars. For a time, the three whaleboats bob like quiet buoys in the ocean.

Finally, a hole is cut in the whale's tremendous flukes; a towing chain is drawn through and fixed. The mate in the waist boat announces the hunt has taken them north; therefore they will put up their flags and tow south. The wind has shifted; the water chops. This is the largest whale they've speared.

They bend to their oars and pull.

To be so out of sight feels unfortunate and foreboding. The *Esther* ought to have followed on the wind, but for some reason did not—perhaps it was the wind's direction that made a difficult tack. They pull into the afternoon. Without any mark to steer by, it seems as though the whale at times is still leading them. The isolation is unbearable—one puts a head down and lifts it to see no progress at all.

To do this for what one hopes will be half a day is bad enough, but soon, a second complication announces itself. To stern, a gray dorsal fin emerges from the water and cuts cleanly across its surface. The men row without speaking. The steerer calls another fin, further away.

Two sharks. The whaling party is not alone.

93.

There is not much to be done. These sharks hold sway over this stretch of water. They are as old as the sea itself—dark, mean ripples under the waves. From a wide circle, they smell the whale, her blood—then, dispiritingly, they close. "Faster," calls the mate, but it won't help. Soon the water near the whale's carcass churns alive, and the men in the boats see the flashing belly of one shark and the sharp teeth of the other.

They cut between the boats under the tow lines. They tug at the whale's beautiful sides. "Begone!" cries the mate, but he is asking a favor that will not be granted.

94.

With some encouragement, the men keep at their oars and pull as hard as they can. The steerer stands to cut one of the sharks with his lance, but the boat is slick and un-steady, with no crotch in the stern to rest his thigh—he misses and falls into the water. This catches the sharks' attention, and the smaller one lunges—but at the very last second loses interest; he closes his gaping jaws right at the steerer's thrashing feet, a warning. The men pull the steerer back aboard, where he drips and shakes until he calms down. "His mouth!" He's had a good look. Past the rows of sharp teeth, it's like staring into God himself.

That they are helpless to stop this theft only makes the men angrier. The whale is theirs, after all. Now and then the ropes draw strongly and heave the boats off course. Then they slack. *It's not fair,* is what they are thinking. One of the sharks jumps near them, flips almost in play.

They row until their backs sing.

95.

Having finally spotted the hunting party, the *Esther* trims her sails and sets a course to meet them. But the wind is wrong, and she is over a mile away. "Hang on!" the mate cries. "Almost there!" But that's a lie. It will be hours still.

By the time whaleboat and ship are reunited, the whale is missing her fins and a chunk of her belly. The men are furious. Twilight is coming on.

And the two sharks have been joined by three others.

96.

Not without difficulty, the tired men fix their bitten whale to the *Esther*. No one wishes to stand on the lowered cutting platform, no more than an unsteady plank held weakly over the waves, while this vicious dance between shark and carcass occurs, but if the sharks are not dealt with, they will take the whale to the bottom of the sea. The guns are ordered unlocked and brought out. The boys thrust them into the mates' hands, who take careful aim. *Boom*. The shooting has little effect—only one of the thrashing creatures, all teeth and wrinkled nose, is hit directly, and he seems less than moved by the thump near his eye. Hold. Swim. Steady. "Again!"

Another shot.

Unbothered, the sharks continue to pluck at the whale's belly like nursing and nuzzling hogs. They are relentless. Small chunks of flesh now float on the water like pale pieces of paper. It looks as though someone, after opening a present, has thoughtlessly discarded its wrapping.

Meanwhile, on the cutting platform, the men slice and peel the blubber as they can. One finally turns from the whale to swing his spade like a sod cutter; he gives a great yell but is too far from the scrum; he slices only air. All can see now that four of the sharks are small and on their own will not cause too much damage. But the fifth is as fat as a barrel—a sharp-swimming jawbone risen from the darkest part of the ocean. Arnold Lovejoy unbuttons his vest. Thule stands beside him. "He's eating your lunch."

The only thing will be to attack.

The whaleboats are once again lowered. This time, with the furious men prepared to fight, it's a one-sided affair. The second mate finds a shark's eye with the tip of his lance and plunges it out. Another man puts a sizable gash in the underbelly of the largest shark.

It is soon over. And one wishes to never think of it again.

98.

Yet, for some on board, the episode *does* linger.

For, once the injured sharks finally retreated from the whale, they began nipping at one another. One gouged his brother, who chomped back, this shark then attacked a third, and so on, with blood flowing freely until, no further than fifty yards from the *Esther*, they came together in a frenzied, vicious scrum. They bit and tore, dove and bit, jumped—their crazed behavior made no sense. Nose to tail they flailed and turned, giving chase—until in the water they formed a loud, thrashing circle, with the whites of their bellies and the gray of their backs making this circle complete. It was like watching a silk umbrella spin on a distant stage.

From the rail, the cook, boys, and cooper had witnessed this uncommon sight. And if not for the company of the others, none would've believed what happened next. For suddenly, not far from where they stood on the *Esther*, the surface of the sea depressed; it went conical and churned in front of them like a gyre, and it was into this deep circle of water the fighting sharks were pulled. Briefly, they formed a pulsing ring of radiant light, which then dispersed as the ocean regained itself and hid them from sight.

This seemed worth commenting on, but none knew what to say. "That could've lit the sky," the cooper finally said.

Meanwhile, the whale was winched back, resecured.

The men peeled her like a grape.

"This ship was theirs you know," Thule says. "Mrs. Ashley birthed three children while at sea. In this very room, in fact. Right where you are sitting." "I did not know that," says Arnold Lovejoy. "You know one of them. He was the one you met in the bar." Thule taps his teeth with one of his fingernails. "He's the one who talked you into taking this voyage." "I see," says Arnold Lovejoy. Thule looks deeply across the table in the cabin's lanternlight; Arnold Lovejoy dims the wick so Thule will not perceive his sudden discomfort. For a long time, neither man speaks.

"The problem you are going to have," Thule finally says, "will come from overthinking the purpose of this expedition. Do not make simple things complex. This bitten whale has rendered poorly. Perhaps it was the sharks, perhaps not—but was she worth stopping for? These depleted creatures are no longer our concern; they've given what they can. To stay on schedule, we need to reach the northern grounds by the opening of summer. The weather will close on us like a dome." "She's sunk," Arnold Lovejoy says. "The *Dromo*. She was crushed. Long ago. She's gone." "What does the tooth tell you?" At this, Lovejoy is silent. "He would not have let all of her sink," says Thule. He closes the door behind him.

Arnold Lovejoy is not sad to see him go.

The boiling begins. The breeze decamps elsewhere.

Darkness creeps over the eastern horizon and settles like a blanket over the lap of the sea.

The *Esther* catches three sperm whales as they swim north on the current, and for four days, the men bend to their work without stopping: they strip, hoist, slice, cook, scoop, barrel, scrub, clean. No one sleeps. The calf they struck was sickly and had nearly sunk, but the other two have full heads. The cooper makes his casks. At night, the *Esther*'s pots push a crackling red fire across the sky. Her free sails droop and hang quietly.

They come alive with jumping shadow.

Every dark corner of the ship now whispers to the boys. *Eastman. Eastman is here.* They've avoided him as they can. If they see him on deck, they stay away; they don't go below alone and keep themselves busy. Entire days pass when it seems as though they have settled and can call forth their time on the ship before he'd cornered them; other days they feel his presence like a black spot on their skin, and it's as though in thought alone they summon him. *Don't speak of it*, they remind each other. *Don't think of it. Imagine a different ship, on a different sea.* But he trails them; they see him over their shoulders; there is nowhere for them to go. Neither knows how to swim.

It seems Eastman for the most part has avoided them, too. Perhaps he is ashamed.

Doubtful.

101.

Something is in fact moving in Eastman now, it's like a wakefulness . . . for a time, he's kept himself below, watching . . . after the episode with the sharks, he'd followed them into the steerage (they were careless); he'd felt his pulse quicken, the eyes of others, and he'd turned away . . . but now, with the men on deck tending to the pots . . . now, as they are waiting for the cooper (where is he?) . . . now he finds them and pulls them into the empty fo'c'sle. The room smells like wet wood and the sleep of men. It's as dark as a catacomb . . . He's surprised the boys don't call out. He can feel their fear. Why don't they call? He understands where he has them, now. "You're upset," he says. "I know this ship better than anyone. Who would believe you? And who would care?" He forces his thumbs into their mouths.

"Bite," he says. They bite and taste his blood. "It's the strangest thing. I don't see you, and then I do. Where do you go? You think you can get away from me, that I would forget, but I simply won't. This is the world now, your world. It flickers and calls, available only to you and me. But you'll say nothing."

He pulls their clothes off and stands before them. He pushes their heads together, holds them ear to ear. He does what he wants, then lets them go.

When the steward rolls the final barrel and stands it end-wise in the hold, Arnold Lovejoy opens the rum. "Mates first, then steerers, then cook, then cooper, then seamen. We'll keep it below." He tells anyone who'll listen to take it with sugar.

Even Thule emerges for the celebration. The men, normally quiet in his company, are exhausted; it's been four days, they are deep into the rum and see no further than that. Why not, they are shipmates after all. No one is much bothered by his presence. "Grim Thule, Grim Thule." A little song. He grins and raises his cup. He understands. The boys are not present. But Eastman's there. His eyes are dull. What was moving in him before now sleeps.

The tropical moon hangs in the sky like a signal lamp, open, not closing, a constant light. The *Esther* will drift for the celebration, for the rest of the evening. Her sails are furled, and she floats on the calm water with bare poles. It's tradition. She is exhausted and recovering as well. The rum goes quickly.

The men stay below, wrestling and singing.

Another cask is opened, and this one puts the men in irons. Gravity comes alive. They go limp and rest next to one another, wicks extinguished. Collectively, they dream of more rum, a greasy ship. A triumphant return. Their mothers and fathers. The smell of trees. One might imagine the scene as an oil painting, hung in a gallery, a moment caught for posterity and for the edification of those locked on land: whalers at ease, asleep, at peace.

And yet!

Had anyone remained awake, he might've glimpsed a different, and far more ghastly, sight. For once the men are finally still, the rum kicked and the galley in disarray—and all other movement below has settled into the memory of movement—a shipworm emerges from the shadows near the stove. He is ancient, black and wet, unnatural; as thick as an anchor's line. He's pulled himself free of the *Esther*'s wood to smell the air. At his full height, he would stand on level with the cook's remaining pig, who, caught finally by sense, shrinks to the back of his pen in fright.

Now another crawls from the wood. They inch slowly among the sleeping men—over their arms, across their resting faces.

With an old patience, they circle the fo'c'sle for an hour until they find a small crack between the *Esther*'s dank, perspiring planks and bore themselves back into a different part of her hold.

Not a single soul stirs.

The boys have waited all night for the men to quiet, and, finally hearing nothing from the galley, now carefully leave their bunks. "Come on," the older boy whispers. They are headed to the whaleboats. On their hips they carry flensing knives, the blades cold to their skin. They are hurt and sore, and they've discussed it: they cannot stay below, this close to the slumbering men, the rum, to Eastman, who might wake. Eastman will not find them in boats, will not think to look there, and if he does, perhaps they will yell, perhaps they will stab him, perhaps, perhaps, perhaps.

Topside, all is quiet.

They climb the davits and look over the ocean. "The water is strange," the younger boy says, wincing; his mouth aches and he cannot not put more words to it than that. The air is thick and heavy, the wind warm. The moon's light cuts through the spars and throws thin shadows across the deck. The ocean is as still as can be, but the water *is* strange. It looks nearly solid, darker than usual, its surface dense and still. "Don't speak," says his brother. "There," the younger boy says, squinting. He's heard a splash in the distance. He points over the water to port. "It's nothing." "Wait."

Then they both hear it: a sucking sound, a quiet splash. Another. In the near distance, they see a wash of green luminescence, as though the sea's surface has been stirred by an oar. "There." The younger boy points again. "A boat?" "No." Finally, he sees what is clear to his brother: not a small boat, but a figure swimming toward them. The figure—a fish?—dives like a dolphin, swims over the waves, then under the dark water, then over again. Neither boy speaks. Closer, closer now. They see it's a man. Or at least, it appears to be.

He surfaces and dives again.

They watch without speaking so as not to draw attention to where they stand near the whaleboats. But when the swimmer reaches the *Esther*, hoisting himself from the water and climbing her hull, scissoring one leg then the other over her rail, he approaches and stands directly before them. Looking at him, they cannot move. Even in the darkness they see his black eyes. And what appears to be a bird's face, with feathers and a long beak, sharp and closed.

He wears no clothes; his body, at least, is like theirs.

Pale, bruised. Though not shivering.

He looks at the boys for some time without moving.

"I've followed you for a great distance. Don't you remember?" he finally says. They do not. Yet as he stands before them, with water pooling at his feet, and they take in his naked and dripping body, knees, jutting hips, with skin like their own from his chest down—they see the feathers on his neck are white, then black around his

avian face. At the base of his dark beak, a streak of red—
and a picture forms. "Oh, yes," the younger boy finally
says. "You've come back."

The visitor bows slowly and clicks his beak.

In one hand he holds the steward's lost and soaked hat.
He stands, wrings it dry, and drops it on deck. "That's the
invitation I was waiting for," he says. At his full height,
he is much larger than either boy. "Now, hold out your
hands," he says. Unthinkingly, they do and into each
palm he places a piece of white sailcloth. "He was not
stitched so well." They bring the scraps close to their own
faces and in the faint moonlight see their names, written
in their own hand. "You had wings," the younger boy
says. "Yes," he says. "I did. But things change." He raises
his arms in front of him and looks at them appraisingly.
"Don't be afraid. You'll see."

They are not afraid. They study the bruise marks and
scratches on his body. Five small punctures, hand, hand,
foot, foot, ribs, just like Eastman had done to them. "You
are like us," the younger boy says. "Not entirely," he
says, and clacks his beak. "Do you have a name?" "Oh
yes. I have many names. You may call me whatever you
please. Give it a try." But neither boy finds he can speak.
Finally, the younger says: "You are Old Sorrel."

"Yes," he says. "Call me that."

With a quick movement he crouches, then stands again.
He wiggles his toes once, twice, as though trying them

out. Then, with a sharp cough, he bends and vomits sea-water from his long beak; it's a huge amount; it gushes all over his feet, and reaches the boys, who don't move. In this new puddle, a small fish, suffocating. "Poor guy," Old Sorrel says.

"Is this a dream?" "Of course not." But the boys are not sure. "If you were dreaming, could I do this?" he says and opens his black throat. *"Krak Krak."* At first, nothing happens. Then, to port, a breach in the water—a sailfish jumps and flashes her fin; she needles the night air with her blue bill not five feet from the *Esther.* As she lands, Old Sorrel draws a tremendous breath; they feel parts of themselves pulled into his body, down his gullet, into his deep lungs. When he exhales, they feel his breath on their faces. The pain goes away. This is not something they could've imagined. It's a magnificent feeling.

"Why did you come?" the younger boy finally says. "Oh," says Old Sorrel. "Many reasons. Old reasons. One reason. One of your friends lost his hat. I've returned it. And I've decided to stay. I'm early." He shakes and stretches once more; at his full height he is as tall as the smith. "I'm here now. I've much to do. I'll be around."

Without another word, he turns and walks briskly across the deck; he moves gracefully in the moonlight, with purpose and familiarity. At the mainmast, he pauses, and places one hand on the mainsheet. "Mark this spot." Then he lowers himself down the steerage companionway and is gone from their sight.

Perhaps they should've been frightened, but as they'd watched him swim toward the *Esther* and emerge from the depths of the ocean itself . . . *I am here*, he'd told them. And in that they heard they were no longer alone . . . "You called him to us," the older one says. They'd felt his breath, could feel it now . . . They'd wanted him to come.

When the sun rises, they are at the rail to greet it.

From his bunk Arnold Lovejoy can hear the barometer slowly scratching its tape. He has not dressed for the morning. Following the celebration, two days of sluggishness: slow progress, moping feet. Each man has had to sweat off his corona of rum pain. To Thule he says: "It is possible to think fondly on a particular point in history as well as despise it."

Says Thule to Arnold Lovejoy: "It is not."

Weeks pass, and the weather does change. One can feel the drop in pressure. Once on deck, Arnold Lovejoy sees the low clouds spreading across the sky. They are deeply gray, ominous. Into that—that's where they are heading. *Snow. Darkness, snow.* He wants to return, for this to be quickly over, happily settled—a life where his letter is received, breathlessly read, taken to bed, and, once there, more slowly appreciated. Bundled below, he traces the contours of her face on the smooth tooth's surface. He doesn't wish to cause embarrassment, but he can't help what he feels. He's compelled. It's physical. His appetite is growing.

He flushes. Soon he imagines her thrill at his letter, holding it close to her chest. She has begun her own composition, addressed to him. It begins: *Never had I thought* . . . And then that universe becomes this one.

With the Aleutians in sight, they dart one more sperm whale; at seventy-five feet, he is close to the largest whale the men have ever seen. With great effort and celebration, they bring him home. In his butchered bowel they find ambergris, his jewel, hidden, now theirs. They work his teeth from his fearsome jaw. Each man receives a tusk from the deep. "Sketch the hunt!" "Sketch a ship!" The teeth are so large one could put a book on ivory. Now, with the skinned carcass still tight on the *Esther* and bobbing enormously with her on the waves, the men chop a line through the whale's thick skull. They lower the boys from the rail to scoop the case.

No one else is small enough.

The whale's head is like a shallow cave: dark, wet, stagnant, still. The cloudy sperm rises above their knees, still warm. To see the whale is one thing; to stand on him, and then within him, quite another. His cut flesh is yellow and slick; and for balance they push their thighs against bone. His head is as large as one of the *Esther*'s whaleboats, and were he not dead and peeled, one could imagine his jaw closing with true power, or his snout butting ship's hull to splinters. But he no longer moves, and the boys climb forward until they stand square in the headcase the men have opened like a giant's wet purse. There is room enough for them to lie down head to toe and rest there as though in a pungent hammock, looking up at the men who line the rail expectantly.

The spermaceti smells like raw milk. They ladle and scoop, send buckets from their dank zone to the surface. Each full bucket is greeted with shouts of encouragement.

107.

Since his arrival, the boys have seen Old Sorrel at the strangest times, in the strangest places. They've spotted him astride the *Esther*'s bowsprit, looking forlornly into the waves, found him sleeping in the raised whaleboats. In the galley, he perches above the stove, and clacks his beak at the unhearing cook. He hangs from the yard and watches as they help the blacksmith at his grindstone. He strides the deck amidst the bustle of men, untying their knots, unseen by all but them.

And sometimes the long days on the water pass without the boys seeing him, or any sign of him, at all.

Yet, even when they cannot see him, they know he is there, and watching—for his presence has settled the ship. Eastman has kept to himself. He does not trail them; he does not look for them, nor so much as turn as they walk by. At night, the boys thank Old Sorrel and wake to the work of the day. The *Esther* is back to her busy routine, and they are relieved and pleased he's come. He sleeps in the darkest part of the *Esther*'s hold, where he's made a home.

There he pecks and peels her copper sheathing, making a nest from the scraps. They hear his loud breath as he works, and to the sound of his scraping fall asleep. Their friend and protector, their visitor alone. They speak of him only to each other.

Now, with the Aleutians in view, Old Sorrel materializes as they scoop the sperm whale's headcase.

He's perched on the tip of the whale's skull, watching them work. The boys are happy to see him. He's been gone for a week. "Hello, hello!" they call.

"Hello!"

But Old Sorrel sits on the whale's dismal head with his arms around his knees, hunched, cold. His back is slouched, his eyes vacant. He does not respond. They continue with their heavy work—the waves make it no easier. They have ropes tied around their waists, and when they tug, they will be hoisted back aboard the ship. "There is no . . ." Old Sorrel begins. He sighs. "I'm not going to be speaking today."

They scrape the whale's junk and fill their buckets halfway. The case is almost empty. It's the last thing to be done before letting the whale sink. "Lie down," Old Sorrel finally says. "Stay here awhile." "In the whale?" "Yes," he says. He's not looking at them. He seems to be talking to himself.

"What is it?" the younger boy asks. But Old Sorrel stays true to his word—he speaks no more. His black eyes glisten as he watches them work. His beak does not move.

Oh, this whale! He had been so beautiful. The boys signal they wish to be pulled up, and when they are hoisted safely out and on deck, the men cheer. The poor whale is now completely stripped; he is only tendon and bone, unrecognizable. They cut the carcass loose.

So huge, and so beautiful.
   Their sails fill, and they leave him, rotting, astern.

High overhead, a patient, hovering gull has been in the air for hours, waiting for the ship to sail off. He circles once more. When the ship is finally away, he folds his wings and lands clumsily on the whale's drifting carcass and begins to peck and pull at his flesh.

He approaches Old Sorrel, still crouched on the tip of whale's snout, unmoving. In his unwavering hand, Old Sorrel holds a small piece of the whale's lung. The gull fluffs his wings, and steps forward to take it. With practiced quickness, Old Sorrel springs the trap—he opens his beak and eats the bird in one gulp.

On the *Esther's* last plunge in the Pacific, Old Sorrel visits their cabin. It's night. He gestures and the boys follow him deep into her hold. "Watch," he says. He holds his fingers in front of his beak. With a quick wiggle he produces a flame and cups it in his hands like an ignis fatuus. "Everything has two handles: one by which it may be carried, the other by which it can't. A wise man once said that." The flame goes blue. Then with frosted breath he blows it out. "Simple." "Do it again!" the boys say. Old Sorrel shakes his head. He inhales deeply and closes his eyes.

The boys look around. From the *Esther*'s stern, they'd seen him eat the gull. They see the new bruises on the human part of his body—dark brown, near his elbow, on his thigh and above his penis. Unlike their own, his wounds have not healed. In one corner, next to his neatly arranged nest, they see he has begun to tie pieces of rope together. "What is it you're making?" Old Sorrel keeps his eyes closed. "A net," he says. "You'll see."

PART
TWO

New Bedford, Bristol Bay, Chukchi Sea,

Farthest North, Pacific Ocean, Southern Tropics

\\\

Arriving Letter, The Clotting Leads, A Frozen Ship,

Expedition Over Ice, An Unexpected Encounter,

Bowhead Birds, The Walrus Hunt, Vengeance of Sorts,

The Breaking of the Ice, Hell of No Interval,

A Treasure Returned

\\\

1879

NINE

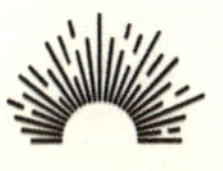

1.

She wants away from the house, and so she wakes early and leaves. In the jangly, misted light, the waterfront is quiet and still, but there is no peace, and Sarah Ashley walks quickly through the wharves until her legs grow tired and she sits to watch the morning unfold. Soon the docks wake and each returning ship is unloaded without hurry. Barrels of oil sit on their ends; men roll them out carefully for counting and set them in endless rows. Baleen is bundled, stacked like firewood, and marked with each ship's name. For a time, when she saw a ship's steward or captain, she'd ask after the *Esther*, and by now she's used to the reply. No ships have seen her, there has been neither gam nor exchange. Yes, they would've remembered a ship rigged in such a way.

It's as though the *Esther* has become a ghost ship. The steward recognizes Sarah Ashley and flushes. He knows of the *Dromo* and of her husband. He knows to whom he is speaking. "How is your father?" he asks. "A fine man." "He is busy," says Sarah Ashley. "He is well." She nods at the barrels he's counting, fewer than usual. "Not a large haul." The steward shrugs and goes sheepish. "You know how it is."

She does know. She reads the papers; she is of this world. Petroleum is cheap as nuts, and its quick extraction has begun calling forth a new age. The railway has connected the oceans, and folds time itself. It's how she's received the letter she now carries in her pocket so quickly. "I'm looking for the *Sophie*." "She's south, past the quay," says the steward. "A full bag of bricks. She's not one of yours, is she?" "Of course not. Thank you." Sarah Ashley turns, raises her hand, and points south. The man who follows her stands two hundred yards away.

He sees her signal. He touches his wide hat.

She is being escorted by one of her father's men. This one rarely speaks; he is like a shadow. He sweeps up and closes doors behind her. He's been there since the *Esther* embarked—when she leaves the house, he follows. That her brothers move around the city unencumbered while she endures such a tether . . . that is her story now. She's grown used it. One forgets about him.

But others don't. When she walks through town with her shadow, people on the street step aside to let her pass. Crowds part like the sea.

The morning tolls its bell. Sarah Ashley looks once more toward the unloading ships, then turns and walks down the wharf.

3.

The *Sophie* sits on a dead corner, true south of the quay, her lines slack and dripping with weeds. Her waterline is green and grown over; barnacles jewel her stem. She's sat on her lines for a year, with nowhere to go, of no use to anyone but the harbor rats. Her rail is stripped; someone has chipped the face off her figurehead. Her poles are bare. No ship does well after such idleness, but it would've been clear to anyone that the *Sophie* had never truly been a beautiful vessel. However, in his letter, Arnold Lovejoy claimed she was—despite her failure, he praised her lines and full sails, the small uplift in her bow. She's come to see for herself.

It's not all he had written, of course.

She'd kept Leander's letters. He'd written from his first voyage of the Galapagos and the seas of Japan—he wrote of the chase, and the feel of the ship; the stories he'd heard. It was what men did. Now, in view of the *Sophie*, she reads Arnold Lovejoy's letter once more. She squints, runs her fingers up the rough edge of the paper. *Pretend*, she thinks, and then she makes it so. She remembers Leander's touch, and his smell. His eagerness to be with her. They are Lovejoy's words, but they call forth Leander, and like a vision, he appears in front of her. "You shouldn't have left," she says. His eyes are vacant. He speaks nothing in return.

5.

It is true that the sea and her family leave nothing untouched. Shortly after her wedding to Leander, she and her father, who had grown too old and busy to captain his own ship, had begun their work. In her husband, her father saw great promise: a young and pliable man who ventured the waves without fear. He took Leander aside; he had given him gifts—irons and luck-charms from his own time on the water. He whispered in his ear. She'd encouraged it. But when Leander returned from his first expedition as captain of the *Dromo*, his eyes had changed. He spoke only of the ocean; he walked on land, but he'd never left the water. Some part of him was absent. When she reached for him, it was like touching cold stone. "What is it?" But he would not answer. She was not naïve. She herself had seen the pictures—the slaughter, the dissection, the desire it provoked. She'd watched as her father bestowed upon him their family's golden heirloom, the hatless man, and hung it around his neck as he embarked for the final time. She knew its draw and its cost. "He'll go again," her father had said. She hadn't wanted him to. But neither Leander nor her father would listen. And when she'd objected, a door was closed in her face.

6.

She'd written to him of their child, his difficult birth and frailty. She wrote of her worries during his long absence, and her regret in involving him with her family. She told him what she wished for: to be free of her family's orbit though she knew such a thing to be impossible. For it had first been her idea to send Leander to sea. These letters she had not sent. The *Dromo* crossed the ocean and entered the ice. Leander wrote to her father of the whales he'd killed and what he'd seen. He wrote that the whales came to him, as though drawn to the *Dromo*'s mast itself. He did not write to her. A season passed, another, and then another. Then he did not write at all.

7.

A gull lands on the *Sophie*'s peeling bowsprit and fluffs his chest. The man behind Sarah Ashley bends, picks up a stone, and tosses it with true anger. It hits the gull on his wing. "No one likes birds on boats," he says. "Even this wreck. It's rude."

"Your child," he finally says.

From her pocket, Sarah Ashley takes the letter and reads it once more. She looks at the *Sophie*, feels a frown forming, and drops the pages into the water. "It's just a gull," she says to her shadow. "Still," he says. The morning is over. She turns and follows him back up the hill to her house.

8.

The curtains in the sitting room are drawn, and the room is dark. She takes off her coat and walks to her son's crib; she picks him up and holds him close. "We tried to feed him," Mrs. Ashley says. "You were gone." "The scrawny boy won't eat a thing," says her father. It is unclear to Sarah Ashley if he's been standing in the corner near the door this whole time, or if he's just walked in.

Her pale child is four years old. He cannot walk, is wilted, and will not speak. "Where is your letter?" Ashley says. She turns to her father. In the dark he looks half-formed and ill. She looks away. "It hardly matters," she says. "He is doing as you asked." "It is not *only* Leander he is looking for," Ashley says. "Not just for your son's sake, but for our family's." "I do not need reminding," she replies. Her father nods once. He coughs and leaves the room.

After some time, Mrs. Ashley approaches her daughter. "Letters arrive from sea, my dear, and their fevered contents might slant your thinking. The effect can be disorienting. Lord knows I have received letters like this, and I can attest to their effect: one feels as though someone has lain a story over your own experience and made it so. But this has turned out better than we had hoped: you are his beacon. He will drive his ship through the ice for you, find what is ours, and return for *you*, and that is what matters." She reaches for her daughter's hair, then pulls away. "You have been born into great luck; that luck must be maintained; and you have done your part. It is a gift is to move through this world as a young woman—as an instrument of this family—if you strike the proper chords, the light will raise itself and you may do then as you please. That this is a world designed by men, for men, is no surprise; yet true strength comes to you when you see your opportunity. It has hardly trapped you. Look around! This house was built by the sea. Nothing weak survives in this world, nor gains respect, nor has what we do, and only the infirm would apologize or agonize over that fact. Sink your doubts. Do not think about them, they have no utility. And if we must abide, then we abide. Do not think of Leander as he was or as you wish him to be. Do not think of anything except what must be done."

Sarah Ashley coughs. Her son wakes and begins to grumble. "I was only remembering," she says.

9.

"I am not unsympathetic," says Mrs. Ashley. "I understand. But you have seen your father losing strength. Your
child can neither walk nor feed himself. The *Esther* is our
last hope. The hatless man has been with our family for
years. It's like a father to all of us. We must have it back."
The door opens, and into the room walk the old riggers.
They are being escorted by her brother. "Give them the
child." "I know, I will." "They will care for him."

Her brother gently takes her child and hands him over
to the three wizened men, who cradle him in their ruined
hands and take him from the room. It has been this way
since the *Esther* departed.

"I know," she says again, and they close the door behind them.

10.

In front of her, a scale model of the *Esther* is set once again. Into the room comes her father.

He has been burning his candles down, and into her hand he presses a cup. "Drink," he says. It's hot on her throat, and smells like ambergris and lavender. It's like tasting light. "Come." She sits facing him and her mother. They put their own empty cups at their feet and reach their hands to one another. The room dims. From the candle in front of them, a blueish light; it dances across each familiar face and gives the whole room a feeling of submergence. She sees, on the ship model before her, small figures, the *Esther*'s crew; they scurry here and there, small shadows, small men.

Scenes are acted out. One man climbs the mast and points north; others, at the rail, hoist a blanket piece of blubber to deck to be chopped. Her father leans his pale face close to the small ship. "I get bored, I cannot help it." "Be patient," her mother says to her father. But he radiates agitation. She's seen him push a man to the deck from the yardarm for no reason at all. She's seen him blow low gusts to their sails, and speak to the small figure of Thule, who has the ear of his captain. But her father has no real power. "Be patient." "I am."

Yet, while her parents watch one part of the ship, she's watched another. She's seen the two boys and the man who is preying on them. And she's seen what her parents haven't: a bird, who's alighted, and now lives in the hold. She's followed his curious progress and not said a word.

"Be patient." "I am." Time barely passes for those on the ship. Her family can only watch. As the *Esther* enters the ice, a fog coats her deck, and they lose sight of the men. It's as though the ship herself is blocking them. "What do you see?" Mrs. Ashley asks her daughter. She says nothing for a while. Then: "Either they will return, or they won't."

As usual, the heavy drink eventually settles in her stomach, and she is sick. "There, there," her mother says. "There, there," says her father.

11.

At night, when the candles are out and her family sleeps, the house speaks to her as it always has. *Do as you must,* it whispers. *Do not complain.* In the letters she's kept, she can still read a younger version of her husband in his lines, he was not yet set on his devouring course; and in them she can see also a life, hers, that has not yet been so fully conscribed, nor aware of the cost of her family's luck. There is a time before all of this when he has not broken himself on the ice; she has not yet sent another unfortunate soul to look for him and bring him home. *Release me,* she thinks. *I no longer wish to be part of this story.* Suddenly, she wishes to scream it. The feeling passes.

Her room is thick with the evening's darkness. It is almost total. *Goodnight,* says the house. *Goodnight,* she replies.

12.

For none in their business can separate from the sea. And it is better to act than to be acted upon. It is possible that a terrible fate awaits each and every one of them, but the voyage has begun and it will be done. *Goodnight,* she thinks. Above her, the ceiling gives way to sky. *Goodnight.* To the whale in the deep, and the ship crushed by ice. To the gulls on the quay, her child somewhere in sleep. To the waves crashing the shore, and a hard wind a lee, to the long wait and winter, all of it, goodnight.

TEN

111.

The men know the *Esther* is approaching the ice; they can tell by the color of the light, which flickers, reflects, becomes at times almost a solid thing. And if even their position had been in doubt, they would know it from the captain's quietness. He's all but disappeared from deck. They are moving away from blue water, and into the white. The wind blows warm no longer. Soon it will be freezing. They've killed their last Pacific whale, and the second part of their journey is upon them.

There is no reason to speak it.

112

This water is old and dark; it's the route the Ashleys wished.

It has been sailed many times, by many ships: whalers have patrolled and plundered these depths and only occasionally come to ruin themselves. The work is long and cold, but the odds favorable, and in general it's a slaughter. In the past, Arnold Lovejoy, standing on deck with ice in view, has imagined himself under the waves—*he* the whale, and *he* the relentlessly pursued. *He*, struck with an iron; *he*, the lung punctured and filled with blood. He'd assumed thinking in such a way was what made a good captain but realizes now that there is nothing special in the approach.

They have weapons and instruments and experience; the whales do not.

"What is it you are thinking of?" Thule says. He sits at the chart table, as he does now that they are near the ice. "Nothing," says Arnold Lovejoy, and closes his eyes. His mind is like a glazed, empty basin; his thoughts come and go. He's put the *Sophie*'s time up here as far away as possible. Thule has helped. Sarah Ashley's face now flashes before him. He blinks and it disappears like air. "Nothing at all."

At night, he thinks of her painting in the hallway. He holds the etched tooth she gave him up in the morning

light. He should not have put into words what he was re-
quired to demonstrate in deed. She'd held everyone at the
party in thrall. Perhaps what he should have done was
take her to the *Esther*, perhaps that's what she, in his ear,
was asking. But what is she asking now?

113.

The *Esther* crosses the Aleutians; she enters the Bering Sea. To port, the Pribhof Islands rise sharply from the water and reach to pointed mountains; the sunset produces a light that plays at their summits like fire cupped by God's own hand. The ocean begins to empty itself of warmth. They are late in the season and see only returning ships, most of whom ride high on the waves. These ships are empty, and Arnold Lovejoy gives them wide berth; there will be no gams.

The men don't mind.

Now, when not on deck, they occasionally sing to one another. The voyage has forced them close. As they prepare for the ice, their voices lift from fo'c'sle: *We've been so foolish, Foolish are we* . . . Why hadn't they signed on to any other ship at all? Why hadn't they hopped off at the tropical isles? A carefree life might have unfolded somewhere warm: a fruit drink, a hammock, the rustle of soft wind. It's a vexing topic of conversation. But they will face the cold and the ice. And they will do the work.

That's what makes them whalemen.

114.

Some days, the fog in the Bering Sea is so heavy it's like sailing through cotton. One can see no farther than a mast's length in any direction.

To navigate, they fire a cannon to hear its echo. Anything at all could be lurking in such weather. In the dim and quiet morning, they listen for whale. "Patience." "Patience." "Ears up!"

They rerig for winter, reinforce the portholes; the deck and hull are inspected for gum. *Wait, wait; soon, soon. Batten the hatches.* That is the song they sing. What the ocean hides, she will eventually reveal.

Snowbirds freckle the sky.

"This fog," says Thule. "It's like sailing through someone's dream, is it not?" Night. Arnold Lovejoy sits at his charts. "It's to be expected. Though I have never seen such thickness myself." "It's Leander. He sends it. He doesn't wish to be found." Arnold Lovejoy marks a depth. "That's . . . ridiculous," he says, and caps his quill.

"It is here, correct?" Thule points to the map. A man on the icepack. In walrus skin. He'd approached the *Sophie* alone and handed Lovejoy his letter. There'd been no ship in sight. "That's correct." "Then we will be there soon."

As they cross the Bering Sea, the cold wind makes music in the halyards, a low drone played in a lower key, and versions of this journey's end begin to root in Arnold Lovejoy's mind. In one, he returns with Leander and the *Dromo*'s cargo and is greeted warmly by the Ashleys. In another, he returns without the husband and the oil, and the voyage's failure will mark him more deeply than he is already marked; he will be rewarded with nothing at all. In another, the *Esther*, herself, gets caught and crushed by the ice, leaving only those with true will to walk across the floes. He hopes above all that his letter will do its work. Likely, the ice has swallowed Leander, and he will not be seen again. It's what the ice does; they will discover it, and there will be nothing to do but push on and return with the *Esther*'s hold barreled to the brim with oil.

Perhaps she will be even more receptive to him then.

"You don't need to visit me all the time," Old Sorrel says. "I'm fine." "We like it down here," says the younger boy. It's not entirely true—the hold is dark and rank; down here it is difficult to see. And they never know what his mood might be. Sometimes he's playful and interested in talking, sometimes silent. Sometimes he's not there at all. But they've noticed that, unlike their own, his body is changing. There are more bruises on his arms. He looks older and winces in pain as he moves. One of the large shipworms crawls from his open beak and sloughs down his body. It works its way between the oil barrels and disappears. "Don't worry about them," Old Sorrel says. "That's where they sleep."

"We dreamed you took us swimming," the older boy says. "You carried us both on your back. We went below the light and couldn't see a thing." At this, Old Sorrel perks up. "How wonderful," he says. "Perhaps, when this is over, we will."

The cook calls for them, and up they go.

118.

On the *Esther* sails through the choppy winter sea! She swoops her sprit up one wave and down another, proud and vain. Finally, the cold truly catches and the temperature drops. The water turns gray and leaden; every surface of the ship remains damp. The fog smothers and surrounds them. But the silence they sail through is not the absence of sound at all. Rather, it is the presence of all sound. The cold bites the men's skin; they feel it in their teeth. They bundle against it, but that's how it is. With everyone so dressed, the boys cannot tell Eastman from a distance.

But he leaves them alone.

They scrape the fallen snow from the deck, pile it up, and sweep it into the water. No one speaks. Salt spray froths and carries up and over the *Esther*'s plunging bow, which, loud and landing flatly on the water, freezes. The boys are set to work chipping ice off the davits—it comes off like a second skin. It is satisfying work. But as the cold deepens and the ice layers, they cannot chip down to the wood. The men wrap themselves in every stitch of wool they own. The *Esther* shivers and holds her beams tight.

Their movement feels like no movement at all.

After a week of this miserable passage work, a favorable wind snaps down from the north and takes the fog with it. That morning, the men have their first glimpse of clustered ice. What a sight! The northern sun glints off the frozen expanse—her light is a dancing thing, it plays over the basin and reflects crystals in the air. The ice cakes are like glistening scraps skimmed from the pots. They see no patch of color in front of them. Everything—sky, snow, apparent horizon—is a gradation of brilliant white. Except, of course, for the sea itself, which, in the leads and channels, appears black.

Having seen this, boys wake Old Sorrel, but he is tucked in and will not stir. "It's like nothing else!" They are hoping to cheer him up. "I've seen it," Old Sorrel says sleepily. He sits. "It's like . . . like . . ." He moves his hands in front of his sharp beak as though trying to pull his thoughts from the air. But no words come to him, and soon he gives up.

The next time they visit they ask:

"How do you control him if he can't see you?"

With Old Sorrel hibernating and hiding, they've been thinking about Eastman. Just because he's stayed away from them doesn't mean he always will. "I whisper in his ear," Old Sorrel replies. "I pretend I'm you. It's a little more complicated, but not much. Don't think on it too long. Just imagine you are on a different ship. This one is three whales below a darting knot. Imagine instead they are martlets." "Yes." "Three martlets. They never alight. I've seen them." "You have?"

"They're magnificent."

But they aren't on a different ship—they are on this one, and some nights, after passing Eastman at the frozen rail, or in the galley, the boys' vision of his scarred back, his sharp hipbone, his terrible penis, returns, and they can't get the feeling of his fingers off their skin. On these nights, the younger boy climbs into his brother's bunk to sleep. At the foot of their bed, they see Old Sorrel. He perches in the shadows, watching them. Black eyes, silent beak. They hear his deep breathing, it calms them, yet he will not answer. They've come to love him, but he will not speak.

E
L
E
V
E
N

122.

In calm weather they clear the straight and sail up a wide channel where ice does not meet land. They pass floes full of sleeping walrus and seal. Each morning the horizon fills with low-flying birds; they dive into the dark water like pelicans and disappear. When they come upon an unmapped island, whose cliffs stretch heavenward, and whose peaks are lit like candles in the afternoon, the men bow their heads and keep to their passage work. In time, the sun reaches no higher in the sky than the *Esther*'s yardarm; her strength is skimmed by the weather; her light is low. She pulses like a distant lantern and, in the evening, washes the ice in a viscous red light. From the deck, it sounds like the ice is speaking to itself.

From the covered rail, Arnold Lovejoy tells Thule, "It's like no time has passed." Thule smiles. "The sea does strange things." Lovejoy nods. Here is where he'd lost two of the *Sophie*'s crew; here, where he'd dropped his father's pocket watch in the dark water; here, where they'd found no whale. He tightens his coat's collar. The *Esther* has sailed through the floes with the greatest of ease, quietly, with deliberation. Ice cakes thump off her reinforced hull without harm. She is built for this. The wind stings his eyes and makes small icicles of his beard. "A ship is an interval," says Thule. "Think only on what's ahead. See what's in front of you. Make it so."

123.

The first mate: "We'll need to move more slowly. The floes are in argument." Arnold Lovejoy nods and gives the order: the *Esther* will keep north and with caution hug the rafting ice. They will soon arrive at the Chukchi Sea, and once there, they will skirt the basin and look for passage even further north: a wide lead, a favorable current that will bring them to Leander.

The cold, unforgiving now, scrapes the inside of the men's noses with an icy finger. They feel it in the roots of their jaws. "But *he* feels nothing." They are speaking of Thule, who has emerged as promised and now spends his days on deck.

124

"The Ashleys are in the tides and the channels now." They form in the faceless clouds, strafing and blowing and urging them on. *Get him, return* is what Arnold Love-joy hears. The *Esther* herself seems drawn north. She sails with a speed he cannot account for. He dreams the charts in his cabin have begun to shimmer and glow like the inscribed tooth itself, which has begun giving off a low, golden light and some heat; he's placed it under lock in his desk. They are getting closer. In the bracing, blank weather, Thule climbs the mast and stands in the crow's nest, his long, dark coat snapping behind him like a blanket. The men give him space. At night, pouring over the charts with Arnold Lovejoy: "We'll be leaving soon." He points to a spot with a long, thin knuckle. "The ice moves erratically. We may be some time." "In *your* experience." "It may snow."

"The wind might howl. But we won't listen."

As expected, the floes stitch together and the ice becomes a continent itself. It stretches north and covers much of the visible sea. In its desire to drift south, it encroaches on the *Esther*'s navigable channel, and narrows it; but the channel does not completely close, and they sail on.

126.

Near Cape Lisburne the men spot a bowhead whale; they lower and lose him.

Over the cold water, they chase another and attach; but the thoughtful and frightened fish pulls the whaleboat toward the ice sheet, forcing the mate to cut the line to avoid being pulled under. The men return to the *Esther* freezing cold and furious.

The problem is one of space. In open water, the whale tires and will eventually surface—it does not matter if he swims them miles from where he's been struck. But in ice-congested water, one does not have such leeway. So, after losing a fifth whale in as many days, one of the mates demonstrates to the assembled men a new technique with a new weapon pulled from the *Esther*'s cabinet: an explosive dart that fires like gun. "For speed's sake. He won't get far at all."

He stands on the cathead and shoulders the lance like a rifle, aiming off the bow at an ice cake. The mechanism kicks and fires, the dart shoots javelin-like and lodges in the ice with a hollow thump—then the explosive triggers and with a *whoomp* sends chunks of ice into the cold air. The men cheer; they've never seen a bomb lance before. It's meaning to them is immediately clear: no more long and dangerous darting excursions in this weather, no more losing whales to the ice.

When they next lower—oars muffled at their fulcrums with matting to soften the sound of their approach—the steerer signals from the chock as he shoulders the darting lance. "On my mark," whispers the mate. The steerer aims and pulls—nothing. They are almost on top of the slow-breathing whale. He aims and pulls again—and with a sharp hiss the ordnance misfires; the dart flashes through his steadying hand, shredding it, and sails wide. The whale dives. One of steerer's fingers lands directly in the mate's lap; the forward-most man, drenched now with the steerer's blood, scampers stern. The bomb itself detonates under the waves and produces a small, harmless burp-bubble on the surface. Disaster.

The steerer is in shock. Slowly, as though in a faint, he tips over the rail and into the water, must be fished out, and for the entire row back, shakes like a kitten, one paw holding the stump of the other, crying tears of disbelief.

Old Sorrel, when told of this calamity, laughs and laughs. "His own hand! It's too much." The boys hadn't thought it funny at all—the mate had lost all his fingers and half of his palm; he screamed for two hours while the captain stitched him up. But he hasn't died. "I can't believe I missed it." He gently wipes a tear from one of his large, black eyes. "Thank you for telling me." The boys exchange glances. They can't quite say it, but since the *Esther* has been in the ice, something in Old Sorrel has deepened, and gone dark. For the life of them, they can't figure out what's caused it or how to help. His legs are the same, as are his arms. He is still, despite the cold, completely nude. A week ago, they caught sight of him on deck, perched on the sprit, covered in snow like a church statue. But since then, he's slept all day in the hold, and rarely leaves. He's sullen, morose. So, yes, it's nice, they suppose, to see him quaking with laughter.

Just as quickly as he's become animated, however, he slouches back in his nest like a snuffed candle.

The boys wait.

They are in the hold when one of the shipworms emerges from between the barrels and twists across the floor. They press themselves against the wall. "He's blind," Old Sorrel says, and claps his beak. "Nothing to worry about." The black worm straightens at the sound of Old Sorrel's voice; it crawls quickly over and fixes its pincers to his hip. A stream of thick, dark liquid streams from the bite; it runs down his leg. "What's it doing?" the younger boy asks. "Just draining the bad blood. Don't mind him."

It's true. The shipworm has bitten directly in the middle of one of Old Sorrel's dark bruises. As they watch, the brown and purple mark slowly disappears. "Then they drink it. It's not as painful as it looks." Another worm appears, this one as thick as a forearm, and begins to lap at the small pool near Old Sorrel's thigh. "This one is ancient and stupid," says Old Sorrel.

The boys no longer wish to stay here, in the hold; but they don't want to appear ungrateful. "I'll see you soon," Old Sorrel says. Hastily, the boys bid him goodnight. He tips his beak to his armpit, closes his eyes, and sleeps.

"We won't be long." In his hand, Thule holds the letter Leander had passed to Arnold Lovejoy. He's carried it all this time. They stand on deck, in the cold. The few men on watch are fastened to their stations without moving. The *Esther* lifts and falls gently, quiet in this quiet latitude. In the letter is written the coordinates where the *Dromo* was crushed and where he intended to live the rest of his days: near a small hunting village that paints an inlet on the northern-most peninsula. "Strange to think she went down here," Lovejoy says. "We are almost directly above her." "Not so strange. Can't you feel it? Look down. Let's greet her." But the water is black, and deep; small ice cakes clop into one another.

There's no telling how deep she lays.

After a week of congested passage work, they see the ice has begun cinching the northern route; it hinges like a gate, blocking the entrance to the Beaufort Sea. They've gone as far as the *Esther* can take them, yet Leander lies farther north. If they are to continue, it will mean abandoning their ship to make their way over the ice on foot. It will take days, a week, who knows; the weather is unpredictable. Arnold Lovejoy to Thule: "This is not how I hoped we would go." Thule, in reply: "Then you should've brought us to the ice earlier in the season. Patience. Endurance. Clarity. Duty. We are walking. We won't be long." "Clearly, you've never walked across ice."

"Oh, yes. Yes, I have."

131.

"Skeptics, listen," says Thule to the assembled.
   "Our aim is true."

132.

Into his pack, Arnold Lovejoy places a compass, his chronometer, two charts, two pairs of wool pants, undergarments, and, wrapped carefully in the cloth that it came in, the whale tooth from Sarah Ashley. The cook packs food and supplies on a sledge they've set on the ice. In the distance, land is visible; the ice will lead them there. It is bad luck to leave his ship, but an agreement is an agreement. He is bound, and he's come this far. "The journey is almost complete," says Thule. He has kept up his argument. He has Lovejoy's ear and watches him closely. The Ashleys depend on you; you have given your word; to turn back now would be folly. "She is counting on you too, you know."

Arnold Lovejoy grants one of the mates charge of the *Esther* and informs him thus: "We are to leave the ship and trek across the ice until we reach land, then we will find the winter depot. Once there, we will decide what to do. Do not stray far. We shan't be long." "Highly unusual." "Nevertheless. The ship is yours."

The *Esther* is to remain in the open channel and fish until they return.

The next morning, fog. This delays their departure. "Perhaps we should reconsider." "Ridiculous." The whale tooth is warm in his hand. Two days later, when the weather is favorable, they leave.

The men gather at the rail to see them off as they hitch their shoulder-harnesses and make their way. Between them they haul a narrow sledge packed high with a tent and supplies. None are envious of this departure and watch as the two men cut a straight line across the floe until they are only dark, hunched outlines against the white. Around them the ice rises in flat shards, like teeth. Now, a southerly wind; it pushes thin snow in swirling rotations across the ice, over and across the *Esther*'s foredeck. The breeze shifts, and the men drop their lines, push off from the floe where they'd anchored, and disperse to tend to the work of the channel.

Their instructions are simple enough—hunt the dark water between ice and land and return with regularity to this exact spot for a sign from the travelers. It bothers them less that their captain has stepped off the ship than when he's decided to do it; it's an issue of time. If their journey takes too long, the channel will close completely and they will be forced to winter over.

Once the sails are set, the men gather near the mast.

"We'll leave before that."

"Won't come to it."

"If it does."

134.

In the morning, the boys find frost on the *Esther's* interior planking near their bunks. One can scratch a crude image on the wood itself. They bundle. Old Sorrel has shown them the new nest he'd made in the ballast hold, where the ship's stem meets her keel. It's in the bow of the ship, dark, tight, directly below the fo'c'sle, where the men sleep. "I knew we were behind schedule, but this seems early," he says when they tell him. "Yesterday. They were rowed to the ice in a whaleboat, they set the sledge. They got out and began walking. They didn't look back once." "Heavenly days." "What do we do?"

"We wait!"

He unfurls a bedroll made of straw and lays a blanket over it. "Come, sit. Do you know the story of the seal people? Or perhaps the fable of the arctic fox and the bear?" The boys do not, and Old Sorrel grows quiet. They sit for a while; he seems satisfied, content with the silence. They, themselves, can think of nothing to say. He does not begin one of the stories. His eyes keep closing and opening, as though he's fighting off sleep. "On second thought," he says. He snaps his beak twice and the light leaves the room. "That's better."

"Do you know what I do?" "No." "I sink ships." "Why?" He snaps his beak again. "Patience, patience."

The men once knew the fable of the fox and the bear, but it's a story they've forgotten long ago. And even if they *had* remembered it . . . For days, the boys wrap themselves tightly and scan the water from the top of the mast. "Orioles, orioles," cries the cook. "What do you see?" Nothing but ice in every direction. An inch of snow covers the deck. Rime forms on the rigging and hangs clear and jagged, making jaws of their footing. In the cold, the *Esther*'s become a quiet ship. They spot a white bear in the distance—he walks without hurry, pays them no mind. Then the ship—she shakes herself free and begins her slow patrol.

One week—early morning as the sun rises—the water churns—birds, they assemble and circle—on deck a muffled call and a cold scramble—in the black water, *right* there . . . In each whaleboat the men quietly ship their oars and hoist the sail. *Hold, hold!* they whisper, downwind in their approach so the polar whale will not catch on.

He exhales lazily and bends his black, glistening back.

As they approach, the men see that this slow whale, enormous and scarred, does not end. He's been struck before. He opens his great mouth to feed on the swarm of krill near the edge of the ice pack. He drinks half the ocean, tongues it back out. The bowhead birds pay him no mind. They chatter away, picking and diving at the reddish slick as well. He makes a slow dive.

When he surfaces, the steerer, bracing thigh to cleat, tosses one dart and then another—they stick—the third he throws overside. The toggle holds and they brace against the cedar planks; the whale runs and dives; the fixed line shoots from its bucket like an angry snake. The men hold their oars, prepared for the pull. But the pull does not come. At first there is confusion. Then: "He's gone straight down!"

This whale, old and wise, has sought the ocean floor. Apprehensive quiet settles in the boats. Perhaps he has no fight to him. He has to breathe at some point; if they are lucky, he will surface within the range of their bomb lances and the kill will be quick. "Did you hayhook him?" "No. He is on the bottom, trying to roll the irons out!"

They wait. The birds, who had scattered at sound of the whale's distress, return. It's a picture of northern quiet. One would like to ask this old whale: What is it like down there, in the belly of the cold ocean? Is it pressure enough? Would one sleep for years?

Then up he comes.

The first charge from the shoulder gun misfires; the next buries near his blowhole and detonates, sending chunks of white flesh into the air. The whale buckles and twists; another bomb is fired. Then another. The sound of the ordnance is deafening; it's the sound that has him upset.

Nothing they are able to do seems to finish him. They surround him in their whaleboats; they poke and cut with their lances now; they churn. Finally, one of the mates pulls the second darting gun from its chest and aims between his black humps; it detonates musically. The whale limply rolls then rights; he begins to swim toward the ice. "Do *not* cut the line!"

This is the end, though; the whale is tired. He does not make it to the ice on this dive and soon he surfaces. The men send one more bomb into his back; this implants and explodes near his blowhole. The bloodied fish, hounded like a snorting bull in a cheering ring, swims on. He slaps his tail to the water with a sound not unlike the detonations themselves.

Finally, one of the men pulls a spade from its harness and slices his flukes where they meet his great body. He cuts until he finds the tendon, then chops with all his might and gets it: a thick spout of blood pushes into the water. The whale opens and closes his enormous mouth, helpless; he can no longer swim.

The next bomb severs his spinal cord and that's what does him in.

The men give room enough to his final throes. His spasms last for ten minutes; finally, he stills. To be sure, one of the boats makes an approach and the mate grinds his spade into the whale's open eye. Dead. They cut a hole in his lip and tie his fins and row him back to the *Esther*, who floats like an iron ship on the horizon, a cut silhouette, dark and visible against the ice.

It takes four men to spade the whale's lip and wrench it up and aboard the *Esther*; another cuts a scarf line around his fin. The blanket piece is hoisted, dripping and white, by windlass. The rope, tight now and yanked, tears the whale's humerus from his shoulder socket; his knuckle bone disjoints and the blanket piece pulls free.

Under the whale's spouts, the steerer threads a head strap and chops with an ax at his upper jaw. The men on deck pull at the windlass and the whale turns in the water; then the steerer hacks the giant's jaw free. His head is thus hoisted aboard and set on deck, where they set about the base of his baleen with chisels. Meanwhile, his hide is peeled by blubber toggle and cut from below.

Next, they turn him so his belly faces the sky. They cut for his tongue and throat; his flukes are sliced into tenderloin. The steam from the men's breath makes it appear as though they are tiny steam engines each chugging through the cold.

Finally, the flayed whale is cut loose. He sinks slowly and with a pillowing ease; a relief perhaps, after all of that, to join the silt at the bottom of the ocean.

In the following days, they find whale after whale raising their snouts to the cold air in full view of the *Esther*. The men find it comical after all their time in the Pacific—"Perhaps they are looking for their brother!" They can't believe their good luck. After weeks of seeing nothing but ice, for their captain to leave them, then this. How to explain that the whales have travelled all this way, all their lives in fact, unmolested? They've made it to the ice, and to those on the *Esther* it's as though they've been trailing the ship. Of course, it's the other way around. It's just that they feel safe up here, where they've never seen ships before.

They lower boat after boat. Each surprised whale is escorted limply back—dead—to be cut, processed.

The fires at midships burn as hot as the sun.

140.

The baleen taken from the whales is stacked near the rail, degummed, and threaded through the rigging to dry.

With her rigging so crowded, the *Esther* appears to the boys less like a ship and more like . . . well, it hardly matters. Though the drying bones looks like feathers, they aren't. The ship hardly flies. The whales have come to her; she needn't travel anywhere at all. Would this ever stop? *No, no,* think the men. The leads that marble the ice are like dark streams, ruptures glinting in the sun. The ice has not yet closed. The steward reports to cheers that the *Esther*'s hold is nearly full.

"He was looking at us. This morning. I could feel it."
"He always looks at us." "This was different. I feel sick."
They've gone searching for Old Sorrel, but he isn't in the
hold. The older boy rubs his brother's back. "You can be
sick." He is. He throws up all over the floor of Old Sorrel's
nest. "Can we stay down here for a while?" "Of course."

Eventually, Old Sorrel materializes and sees what's happened. He steps out of his room, bowing his head now.
He returns with a mop. "What's this?" He's bent to pick
up a square piece of something from the mess. He holds it
up to the light. It's a piece of whale skin. "Well. You must
feel better." Old Sorrel snaps his beak. But both boys are
horrified. Old Sorrel tosses the old piece of skin into a
dark corner and walks to where they are sitting.

"Stay here. I'll be back."

142.

This is a dream within a dream, Eastman thinks.

His heart has been stirred by the image of the younger boy, and before he'd awakened in the fo'c'sle, he had in fact been dreaming of him. He is going to step; he is going to dress and find them. But now it seems as there's a great weight on his chest and he cannot move.

The more he struggles, the heavier the weight grows. He gazes at the space above his chest where he feels the weight, where he is pinned. He sees nothing but the darkness of the fo'c'sle.

143.

Old Sorrel can see Eastman with ease, however; his thick hands, his compulsion. He sits directly on Eastman's sternum, slowly opening and closing his enormous beak. He sees Eastman's black heart, and its black ventricles. They are nothing but earthworms to him.

He also sees a dark cavity opening and closing under Eastman's lungs. It's a mean aperture; he hasn't seen anything like it in years. "Don't move," he whispers. Eastman complies.

144.

Slowly, cautiously, Eastman drifts through his own thoughts. He dreams he is approached by a child surrounded by a flock of birds. The birds lift him from the ground, and drop him, then depart, leaving only the child, a boy, nude in front of him. But no matter what Eastman does, no matter how many times he hits him, touches him, stabs him, he will not fall.

145.

"We live now in the Chukchi Sea." Their passage narrows.

To gaze at the ice from the rail—it's like watching opportunity close. The frozen sheet is nearly endless. From the top of the mast, the boys find they can scan north or south, it makes no difference, all is grayish white. The wind gnashes her winter teeth; she curls and sweeps beautifully over the ice, glossing it dark. For an hour a day, the ice itself is a prism: it captures the low light, warms it, holds it close.

The snow falls. It's like you are in a kitchen, and someone is sugaring a board. It makes that same sound.

The man in front of him has blood on his clothes, and the mate is confused. "The lance hit where?" "Directly . . . on his head, sir." "Lord. Is he dead?" The seaman frowns, clasps his hands tightly. "It exploded. His head is gone."

It's been hard to get even this from him; he's escorted, shaking, below. The story, as far as anyone not in the whaleboat can piece together, is this: They'd spotted a whale and lowered, rowed for two miles near the rafting ice, pulled up quietly behind him. Then a misfire, or a mistime, or perhaps he stood when he shouldn't have, or perhaps the steerer slipped. The result is a dead man, all shoulders now, no head; they've left him in the whaleboat, rafted to the *Esther.* "Right, right," the mate says quietly.

"His blood's froze by now." Two men lift him from the whaleboat nearly despondent. The boys are sent to clean. They chip at the gunwale with chisels and drop the loose pieces of scalp and hair over the side; they sluice the seat with warm water. It's quickly done.

The dead whaleman is rolled in canvas and tied, weighted at the ankles. The mate quickly blesses his headless body; he says the man's name. He has no mouth to sew. They tip him over the rail and in. He plunges like a wrapped rug into the cold water with a slap. But he doesn't sink. The canvas has been too tightly secured; the trapped air keeps his body afloat. He turns slow circles on the surface near the bilge. "For Godsake!" The current gets ahold of the body and pushes it back to the ship; it knocks into the *Esther*'s hull at her waterline. It appears to all standing on deck that the headless man does not want to sink, or be disposed of; he wishes, in death, to come back aboard. He needs his head. Or at the very least, he does not care to be left to the fish.

One of the men fetches a long spade from the deck and slices gently at the airtight canvas shroud from the rail. The suit releases its air. The headless man's body slowly follows his feet. Then, as though tugged violently from below, he disappears into the dark sea. All in the whale-boat agree: nothing more could've been done, it was a terrible accident. The gun had gone off prematurely, with the lance itself narrowly missing two others before lodging in the back of this man's head. Then came the detonation.

The steerer who shot the dart is shunned. He spends the day wrapped tightly in the cold near the *Esther*'s bow. "No more luck like this."

147.

"What has the heart of an eagle, the brains of a muskox, the speed of a grass finch, and the patience of an elephant seal?" says Old Sorrel. The boys think about it but can come up with no answer. "Mull it over!" he says. "It's winter now, you'll have the time."

Soon, and without marking the *Esther*, the Chukchi Sea wins its argument—its ice presses its edges, groans, sifts, slips. In the pressurized, white distance, the floes form ridges. The ice braces and buckles. They will find no more whale.

The men see this jagged ridge and tack south, but they are too late: the northern and southern channels have fused and the path to the Bering Strait has already stitched behind them. In preparation, they trim and fold sails; they redistribute the *Esther*'s ballast and loosen the rigging. Their ocean is nothing but a large lake in the ice; one sees no path north and no path south. And soon the lake itself will shrink.

To winter safely, they will need to raft the *Esther* to the ice, something to be avoided as long as possible. "How did this happen?" the mate says. "You are so stupid," comes the unclaimed response. There is nothing to be done. They've missed their chance and the ice has them now. Either the floes will gather around the *Esther*'s hull and crush her to matchsticks, or by some movement none can control or divine, she will be spared. But they have time yet.

Snow falls, each flake the size of a shaken petal—it's an extraordinary sight.

"You don't feel cold?" the boys ask Old Sorrel. "No," he says. "I don't." "You don't feel the wind?" Old Sorrel shakes his beak. They ask: What's it like at the bottom of the sea? Quiet. Can you walk on land? No. Do you have a mother? Not that I can remember. "You aren't ever hungry?" Old Sorrel sits up. "*That* I do feel," he says. He looks at the boys and laughs.

"How long will we be stuck in the ice?" "Not long." "Will they be returning soon?" "Oh, yes." "How do you know?" "I . . . I know everything!" says Old Sorrel.

They've come to believe it's true that he knows everything. But they want to test him. "What did our mother look like?" the younger one says. "What a wonderful question," says Old Sorrel. "She looked just like you."

And with that, he flips his beak against a barrel's iron band. A spark lights the hold and produces a puff of smoke. In this smoke, the boys see the image of a woman's pale and round face. She looks tired. Kind. She is singing a song. *Let God's bosom be your pillow* . . . The boys begin to weep.

"*Krak Krak,*" Old Sorrel says, and then it's dark again.

150.

He waits for the boys to compose themselves. When they do, they see he's closed his eyes. "What would you eat to stay alive?" he asks. "Tallow? Shoe leather?" "How long without food?" "As long as it takes." They don't have an answer. Their minds have gone blank. "You would eat both," says Old Sorrel. Suddenly they are frightened. "Is that how this ends?" they ask. "No, no," Old Sorrel says. "I'm just remembering old stories."

They see he's finished his net. It now sits folded neatly in the dark corner near the *Esther*'s stem, where the ship-worms crawl through it as though it's a piece of old cheese.

After days of silence, he decides to tell them another one of his stories. *Once upon a time*, he begins. But the story is obscure and detailed, and as they grow tired, they find they can no longer follow it. When they wake, it seems as though they've become part of the story themselves. The *Esther* is too, and so are the men. Every animal in the ocean watches them closely.

Soon, they understand Old Sorrel is speaking of the captain and Thule. "They're approaching a hut. They know they are close. One of them is confused about what he is doing and is doing so for reasons not his own, outside of his understanding. The other moves with great certainty. They have walked silently for miles." "Over the ice?" the older boy says.

"Yes," Old Sorrel says.

"Tell me," he says, "what do you see?" "Darkness," the younger boy replies. Old Sorrel is pleased. "Yes," he says. He stretches his arms over his head and lies down. "I see that, too. But I also see something else." "What is it?"

"Be patient," he says. "When the time is right."

152.

One final morning a migration darkens the sky. These birds swoop near the *Esther*'s spars, a fleet come from nowhere. In quiet movement, they dive and pull fish from the shrinking sea. Tired of waiting, the men watch this coordinated flock, surprised by their numbers. Once one pulls a fish, he hoists him high, circling into the air. The birds change direction; they dart here and there as a family. They manifest a single dark thought. "Begone!" screams the mate. The cook is beside himself below. The silver scales of the fish fleck like tiny mirrors overhead.

From a great height, the fish are dropped and fall from the sky. Only a few hit the deck of the *Esther*; the rest are knocked senseless on the floes. The men cover their heads. The stunned fish lay terrified on the ice and on the *Esther*'s deck, gasping like old, broken instruments.

The voyage has reached its hinge—the weather is a physical thing, bearing through their clothing, touching their skin. Their blankets freeze. The cold needles their skulls; the ship feels small and close. To be in this temperature is to be reminded that one is a body only, and the pain of understanding this stays with men forever. One never quite recovers. It is clear, though, given the drift of the ice, that a few more weeks is all they have before they are sealed in for the rest of the winter. "We should've left," the cook says. No one responds.

How do they appear to these birds, locked in their ship, unable to move freely? And what has been the point? There will be no answers. As quickly as the birds arrived, they fly off, back into the low clouds and are seen no more. No one has seen anything like it. The men scoop the fish they can, but no one is heartened by the incident.

They watch the ice and wait.

The fish stop moving.

They wait still.

TWELVE

1.

They pull the sledge between them, hoisting it with great difficulty up each white ridge and carefully letting it loose to lead down the other side. At the top of these ridges is a view more beautiful and terrifying than one might imagine; the world is without color. The white horizon meets the sky, and where one changes to the other there is no visible seam. "We've reached land again," Thule says. Arnold Lovejoy looks. Sure enough. What he's thought in his delirium to be figments of his imagination, tall snowed-upon statues in an ancient kingdom, he now recognizes as trees.

2.

The cold on his face is magnificent. He's felt unwell for days. When they rest, Thule tends to him in their tent. Thule, wrapped completely in furs, Thule, unblinking. Now, Thule pulls his arm to get his attention. "There," he says and points. Arnold Lovejoy looks and sees nothing at all. There's something wrong with his vision; his eyes won't focus. "There?" "Yes," says Thule. "The depot." He pushes his hood from his face. Time has evaporated; they've been walking for what feels like weeks. "Where?" he says. And then he sees it too: a structure of wood, brown against white, erupting and jutting from the terrain they've just trekked.

3.

The hut is made from the wood of the *Dromo*. Her roof is secured by her salvaged elbows; her planking stacked vertically. Her sprit, propped up and supported by casks, joins one of the hut's walls; from their distance, it gives the whole side of this depot the appearance of a ship's frozen prow, bound by land and dripping with ice. It points north. Upturned pots frame the door; they are like metallic, bulbing growths, blooming from the earth.

4.

"He's not here," Arnold Lovejoy says.

A sharp chimney, no smoke; her lights are dark. She is partly draped in a blanket of snow. Thule grunts. "Let's turn around, then, shall we?" That isn't what he'd meant. "That's not what I meant," he clarifies. He holds the present he has for Leander in a pocket close to his heart. He's grown attached to its purpose; giving it up will be difficult. But he is relieved the walking is nearly over. As they prepare for the final stage of their journey, the clouds in the distance begin to sound a kettledrum complaint. The fog that has been chasing them hushes now, catches up. At first, it's like a fine gauze pulled across their vision. But soon the gauze thickens and it's like staring into milk. The temperature drops. They draw their hoods tight, hoist their sledge harness, and trudge the remaining distance to the hut. "Again," says Thule. "Note it was I who brought us here. If he is not inside, we will wait."

5.

Indeed, it is Thule who has delivered them to Leander, but how he's done so over the ice makes little sense. From the *Esther*, they'd reached land without difficulty. Once there, Thule had stepped off again, adjusted their course, and skirted the shore as they trekked north; and for the duration, they'd kept to the floes. Each morning, on the ice outside their tent, Thule raised his arm directly forward. A shift to the right, then to the left, arm outstretched as though sighting a rifle, reaching with his straight hand toward something Arnold Lovejoy could not see. "There," he'd say, and begin walking his line.

With each step Lovejoy had grown more lightheaded and lost. Was the ship behind them to the south or to the west? Occasionally he'd spotted a low yellow light pulse in the distance, a warm beacon, and became convinced it was to that Thule was pointing and leading them. At night, the golden light was in his dreams: a weak sun, hung above them in the winter sky, watching their incremental progress. They'd never reached it, soon it faded altogether, but each day Thule set out with more certainty, as though his gloved fingers were the brass needle of a compass. At night, exhausted, he'd gaze into the heat produced by their small stove and allow his thoughts to roam.

Thule in the shadows of their tent; Thule asking for and holding the present from Sarah Ashley, as though the tooth were his. Thule humming quietly in the morning, his thin nose and taut mouth. His forehead was knotted and looked like the brain meat of chestnuts. He rarely spoke. Within Lovejoy's chest, a constriction; something growing; he felt old in his cheeks and in his legs. Increasingly, he'd struggled to keep pace. Thule waited patiently. The stars hung in the sky like anchor lights. Time slipped from his understanding.

And the further they'd walked from the *Esther*, the stranger and more instrumental his thoughts became; they fell in with his crunching steps. I am a blood machine; I have lived before and will again. My heart feeds my brain; I've wrapped my feet and hands tightly so that no skin is exposed; my skin is the thin membrane that prevents my liquid from spilling out; it is what gives me shape. Was this Thule in his ear? He didn't know. The wind whipped at his ankles, reared up, and hit him straight in the face. It was like conversing with someone who only talks and never listens.

When cold, he arranged the whale's tooth he'd been given so Sarah Ashley's face pressed his heart. When quiet, he held it and heard her encouragement, clear as a bell, chime across his thoughts. He thought: there is a time when all of this stops. But the cognitive impossibility of such a moment asserted itself. On the ice he found only the cold and the straight line behind them. He'd thought: we cannot stop; that is a pure fact. In their final days, the floes appeared endless, fused in their formation of a frozen continent.

6.

"You've done this before," he'd said to Thule near the end. "Oh, yes," Thule replied. The vista was expansive and stifling, unwelcoming, indifferent—and with each night in the tent it seemed that rather than heading in any particular direction, they were simply attempting to leave one realm of thought in order to enter another. While they dreamt of darkness, the ice waited patiently; when they woke, without speaking they began again. The northern sun watched their slow progress like a burnished, unwavering eye; it was giant, cycloptic; unsetting. The ice cracked and groaned. It spoke of itself as they walked, a long story of warning and comfort, the occasional threat. Night was a blink. It pushed them on. When the wind kicked and brushed the air with snow, the light filtered through in sharp fingers that played in Arnold Lovejoy's mind like music.

7.

Inside the dark *Dromo*, the two of them. The storm is upon them, now, blown down from some disquiet even farther north: It whistles, calms, changes direction. It pulls at the hut's roof with a rough slap.

They call through the fog for Leander and receive no response. In the morning, Thule lights the fire and keeps it stoked with old planks from the *Dromo*. They are careful as they eat what they've carried. Thule does not sleep. He sits cross-legged in front of the fire. When Lovejoy rouses again, they eat. On the dark interior walls, someone has stitched walrus skin for insulation. A brass ship's clock, nailed at eye level, hangs frozen. Above the fireplace there are three mounted seal heads. Three chairs sit in the middle of the room, facing each other. Thule stands and winds the clock. It chimes with clarity and ease.

8.

"How long will we stay?" Arnold Lovejoy asks. His mouth is dry. It feels entirely like a sore. "Until the weather clears," Thule replies. "Or until he returns. He knows we are here. I have delivered you, we have arrived. He will appear. And you, in time, will deliver him."

Gently, Thule reaches to Arnold Lovejoy's breast pocket and retrieves the whale tooth; he brings it close. "What do you see?" He sets it upon a table in front of Lovejoy and watches him. "It has not changed," Lovejoy says. "Three whales, a darting knot. Her portrait. I have memorized the rest." "Let me hear it," says Thule. But Lovejoy won't answer. "We will leave it here until he arrives," Thule says. "Rest."

He does. In the morning, he trembles awake and sleeps fitfully throughout the day; when lying down, he peels layers from his body. Thule watches. When Lovejoy wakes, Thule is close, offering a damp towel. He stands quietly in the corner of the room, his arms outstretched like a bird drying his wings in the sun. He leaves through the hut's door, returns crusted with ice. The moon winks on and off. Lovejoy holds himself between the chimes of the ships clock, which toll unexpectedly. He no longer trusts his own thoughts. He places the whale's tooth on his sweat-soaked pillow so he can hear it speak to him. When he wakes, Thule has moved it back to the table.

In the fire Thule's lit, Arnold Lovejoy glimpses scenes from far away: A wharf with ships unloading, a small city at night. He watches the men aboard the *Esther* calculate their shrinking passage; sees them huddled and unmoving belowdecks. A polar whale dives under the ice; he sees the light of that creature disintegrate and give way to the water's darkness. He sleeps. When he wakes, in the strange embers he sees Mrs. Ashley. She's in the sitting room where he'd been received, her eyes fixed on the ceiling, motionless in a straight-backed chair. Ashley stands behind her, one hand on her stiff shoulder, the other clenched in a tight fist. Across from them is their daughter, as beautiful as he remembers, her features as cut and thin as the etching he's clutched so near his heart. *I've made it*, he wishes to tell her. *I am here.* But in the fire, he observes now that her mouth is turned down; and in the candlelight of their sitting room her eyes are clouded and black, without iris, and she carefully rests her hands in her lap. "They're waiting," he says to the room. "They are," replies Thule. He presses a cup into Lovejoy's hand. "Why else would we be here?" "Is it just Leander they want?"

"No," he says. "Of course not. Go back to sleep."

In his delirium, Arnold Lovejoy dreams of a white bear on the ice, approaching the *Dromo* with the languor of an animal unafraid. He is large, his fur matted, yellowing with age at the ends. His eyes are bloodshot. "It's Leander," he says to the dark room. "He is coming." But the room is empty, Thule nowhere to be found. In the morning, through the *Dromo*'s portholes, Arnold Lovejoy can see nothing but a canvas of white. When Thule returns, he's covered in snow. "You're weeping," Thule says. "You think you are dying, but you're not." "Beyond this there is, what, more snow? Nothing?" Thule chews a piece of salt horse, thoughtfully. "You'd have to see for yourself." In the fire, a squid snaps his enormous beak, settles near a gray rock, and changes to the color of stone. When he wakes again, he sees a figure, dressed head to toe in white fur, standing in the center of the room, warming his enormous hands at the flames.

11.

Even in his fever, Arnold Lovejoy recognizes him. "Leander." The man turns. He wears a square beard like Lovejoy's own, but his eyes are sunken and fierce, the color of snow. "How did you find me?" "We followed your letter." Leander frowns. Slowly, he removes his fur coat, folds it, and places it at his feet in front of him. He still wears his captain's coat. Carefully, he removes that as well. The three seal heads watch as he rolls the sleeves of his woolen shirt to his elbows. "I sent no letter."

"You gave it to me," Lovejoy says. "Yourself."

Leander laughs. "I would remember."

12.

"Old friend," says Thule to Leander. "We have travelled so far." The three have taken their seats, and now face one another in the middle of the room. The chairs are cut from rough wood and uncomfortable. Arnold Lovejoy doesn't remember standing, walking to the chair, sitting. He closes his eyes, opens them; he's focused now. "You shouldn't have," Leander says. "You've come all this way. Who helped you? You would not have found me, otherwise." "We received no help. We rounded the world, entered the ice, and here we are." "How goes it in New Bedford?" "Not well." "I'd imagine."

"Is it true that you've taken another wife?"
   "It is. She's dead."
   "The pain you've caused is unearthly."
   Leander crosses his legs. "You don't know the half of it."

13.

"Now you are here," speaks Leander. "What do you think of my winter quarters? It's taken me years, years, years." "I'd rather be anywhere else," Thule replies. "Simple timbers don't make a ship." In the silence that follows, Arnold Lovejoy feels for the whale-tooth in his breast pocket; he reaches for it, grasps its tip; he does not want to give it up. Leander turns to him. "You've come all this way," he finally says. "As a guest, I hope you've been comfortable. It's a long and arduous journey, I've made it myself. You have not traveled for nothing. What is it you have to tell me? What is it you want?" Arnold Lovejoy, sick man, it is your moment, speak! "We want what is left of the *Dromo*'s cargo." "There is none." "We want you to return with us." "But I come in many forms, now. I am not even myself."

"We want what you carry with you," says Thule.

"Now that," says Leander, "makes a little more sense."

14.

But surely, you knew that to you he would give noth-ing, says the *Dromo*. To me, specifically? asks Thule. To you, specifically, is the house's reply. Leander stands and crosses the room. At the fire, he claps his hands for warmth, and as he turns it seems to Lovejoy as though he's changing, is both sitting and standing at once. The room has filled with his musky smell. He fixes his pale eyes on the seated Thule. "What you must understand," he finally says. "What you must understand and relay is that there is no cooped cargo left, nothing of mate-rial value from the *Dromo*'s final voyage. All of it was crushed. What was not squeezed by the ice, in a fever I opened and poured back in the sea. I instructed my men to unbung all barrels and they did so. We had taken what we wished. Once we were stopped, we returned whale to whale. My men had faith that we would find a new ship and resume our luck, but our fortune stank—returning it wasn't enough—and they died. Every one of them. Con-vey this. I am at peace here. I miss nothing of my old life. Convey this. There is nothing else. Convey."

"Doubtful," says Thule.

Leander laughs. "Let me speak to your friend."

"The man you don't recognize?"

"Yes, he."

Thule sighs. He steps out of the hut and is gone.

15

"My legs have left me," says Arnold Lovejoy. "I have no strength to stand." He feels the room tilt as though in swell. Alone with Leander, he is aware that he has no weapon, nor is in any shape to defend himself. "I don't understand," he says. "That's not true," Leander says. "You've been misled, but its's not true that you don't understand. For example, you know my father-in-law and my wife, for they've employed you. You know you came here by treacherous sea. You know you are sitting in the cabin of my ship. You know that the man out there, your companion, is barely a man. You know that your crew will in time turn against you—they will leave on your ship, and you will die here with me." "No." "But, you do," Leander says. "She chose you. They all did. This gentleman, this old friend who now stands outside, he could not have come here himself. He can command no vessel. He can only attach. You have done what they asked. What have you asked in return?"

Lovejoy shakes his head. "You have a son. You have a wife." Leander's great mouth turns at its corners. "Unconvincing."

From his coat, Lovejoy pulls the whale's tooth and reaches it toward Leander. "What if I accept?" he says. "I do not know," says Lovejoy.

"Have you been swift? Have you been careful? Have you been true?" "I have." "Have you known what it means

to sail under a sun in the shape of a darting knot?" "I
have sailed my entire life." "Then," Leander finally says,
"I urge you to look again at this present." He does. To his
horror and surprise, he sees that the tooth he holds in his
hand has none of the markings he once held so dear. No
whales, no knot. No etching. He turns it over. It's completely blank. "That's more like it," Leander says, and
steps across the room. "There are fools everywhere. It's
not *me* they miss. Nor can I be everything you've wished
for. Watch closely."

With one huge hand, Leander reaches to his own face,
pats the bristles of his own beard, and opens his mouth.
All the teeth in his deep gums are black. He leans closer
and opens wide enough that Arnold Lovejoy can see
down his dark gullet. With his fingers, Leander grips one
of his front teeth and yanks; a sucking sound; it loosens
and releases its root. He straightens and holds the tooth in
his palm, studying it.

A small amount of blood flecks his beard.

16.

It's time to move. Arnold Lovejoy kicks his legs with the force he can muster; still, he finds he has no strength to stand. The *Dromo*'s walls hold him to his seat; clamped arms, clamped lap. The now blank whale tooth he'd carried falls from his lap to the floor like a stone. Leander smiles. "Be patient," he says. He places his rough fingers back to the bleeding gape of his mouth and begins to pull the rest of his teeth out one by one.

Arnold Lovejoy says not one word.

When he's finished, he walks to where Arnold Lovejoy sits and holds open his cupped hand. The dark teeth in his calloused palm are sharp and rooted as the floes they crossed over. He cradles them as though they are valuable coins. "Behold," Leander says. His mouth is a grinning cave. Arnold Lovejoy looks at Leander's outstretched hand and what he sees makes his stomach turn. The teeth are *not* black. They are *not* dark from illness. Each has been scrimshawed intricately. "That . . . makes no sense," Arnold Lovejoy says. "And yet," Leander replies, and spits blood on the floor. He roots through his teeth with a thick finger.

"And yet."

17.

"Each will help you form a picture in your mind. This one is from when we got stuck in the ice." He holds the tooth up in the firelight. "This is from when we eradicated walrus from the floes. This is from when we found an entire village starved because of what we'd done—it was their food, don't you know. I did. Only one boy survived. We were in bad shape ourselves. He took us to another village, where we were clothed and fed, and in that way, through kindness, brought back to life. This is one of my new wife, whom I found in that village." He shakes his hand to shuffle the teeth; they make small clicking sound. "This is from when we poisoned all the men in the village, because we couldn't help ourselves. This one's of the children we turned out in winter. This is the women we disposed of. This one depicts two giants, who came from even further north, they were men who changed into bears. This one is beautifully done: this is a bear hunt. Look at that perspective! That's harder than you think it might be, to render intricately like that. This one marks the moment we said goodbye to the sun. This one is my men slowly starving to death. This is them beginning to eat one another." Shuffle. "This is me hoisting the *Dromo*'s planking all the way up here. Here is a depiction of what my family wants and will not find. This one is my wife dying." Shuffle. "This one is the *Esther*," Leander finally says. "And this one is you."

"That . . . looks nothing like me," Arnold Lovejoy says.

Leander chomps his gums. "Give it time!" he says. He

laughs like he's never heard anything so funny. "I didn't look like this either. But there is nothing up here. There is nothing more in the sea. We've taken it all. The heirloom your friend seeks will not help. It's made me what I am; I heeded its call and embraced its compulsion. It's a part of me now. I have done so much and there was nothing to stop me. It's what men like us do. We do it for others, we do it for ourselves, perhaps. But we are purely instrumental; part of history pushing forward. You'll see it. One changes." Arnold Lovejoy nods at the gift from Sarah Lovejoy, sitting blankly at his feet. "I am supposed to give that to you."

"Keep it," he says.

18.

"You said your men died on the ice."

"They did. It just took some time." With a giant finger, Leander pushes through the teeth in his hand, looking for something. "Here he is, your friend Thule. This one's older, you can tell from his eyes. But see? That's all, that was the last one. Like I told you, no letter."

19

Thule, with snow on his shoulders, reappears. "What did I miss?" he asks. In his hand he holds a leaning knife. Leander laughs and turns. "My mind will not change. I wished to be left alone. I've brought myself up here to think."

"But you have in your possession something that isn't yours."

"And what is that?"

"Don't be stupid," says Thule.

"You can take these illustrations back, if you like," says Leander, dropping his teeth in Arnold Lovejoy's lap. "The written log of the *Dromo* will tell one story; these, if arranged correctly, tell a second one, more pure." The marked teeth are still warm; they click on his legs and tumble like dice. Then Leander holds his open hand out in Thule's general direction. "I swallowed what you came for. You'll have to dig it out."

Thule sighs. "Such puzzlement," he says. "Shall I assume you are not returning with us?" "That is a safe assumption," Leander says. "Unfortunate," Thule says. "Are you ready, then?"

"I am."

With a movement so quick Arnold Lovejoy isn't even sure he's seen it, Thule closes the space between himself and the fire and stabs Leander clean through the neck. There is a blood gurgle; a series of small pops; for a minute, Leander hangs suspended with the leaning knife pinned across his throat. Thule steps gingerly aside; he whips his knife back to its sheath; and the large, bearded man closes his eyes, opens his dark, empty mouth, and drops.

20.

Lovejoy's vision leaves him. When he wakes, he sees Thule has stripped Leander of his clothes and is now looking at his enormous body with curiosity. "I'm sure, in some way, that was a relief to him. But where, oh where, did all this hair come from?" he wonders. Blood is everywhere. He turns to Lovejoy. "It's in his guts," he says. "I don't think I can help you," Lovejoy says.

Thule rolls up his sleeves. "Of course you can't."

21

He watches as Thule presses his palm to Leander's stomach, prodding it delicately with his fingers. He places his ear near his hip as though listening for something. Then he sits on his haunches, draws up his knife, and, with a quick exhalation, buries it square at the bottom of Leander's ribcage and sets about unseaming his belly with precise, violent sawing motions. A putrid smell in the room; it's fetid, foul; a body embarrassed and surprised to be opened in such a way. With a grunt, Thule plunges his hands into Leander's stomach cavity. The wet sounds make Arnold Lovejoy's mouth sour; he looks away. He can hear Thule as he squeezes his submerged fists, rooting and tugging, his breathing loud and labored. One of Leander's feet twitches, making a boot-sound on the wooden floor.

"There. In his tract," Thule says.

He closes his eyes and lets his hands lead him. "Got it," he says. With all his might he wrenches his arm, relaxes to brace, and wrenches again; at the third tremendous exertion, Leander's body gives to Thule what he has been seeking.

"There it is. There, there, there." He sits down next to Leander's body and wipes his foul hands on his shirt. He raises his right hand up to the fire so Arnold Lovejoy can see what he holds. It's an egg-shaped stone. When Arnold Lovejoy looks more closely, he sees it's made of gold.

22.

"What is it?" he says.

"It belongs to the Ashleys," Thule says.

"I've seen it before. In a painting in their hallway."

"That sounds about right."

Arnold Lovejoy, still feeling faint, can think of nothing else to say. "Now we can go," Thule says, and stands. "That is, if your head is clear."

23.

The *Dromo's* timber has held its oil. And though it's wet and bitter cold as Thule and Arnold Lovejoy make their preparations, when they set a torch to Leander's hut it roars a tall, creasing swell of flame across the winter sky. The sound is like a thousand people talking at once; a busy evening gathering; a wall of heat. Arnold Lovejoy has seen whaleboats burned at anchor—a spilled pot, a kicked ember, some crumbling mortar in the works and a ship will light up and sink.

But he's never seen one burn like this.

Thule bends to the ground and rubs his hands in the snow. Between them sits the sledge. They've taken Leander's food, the ship's clock, and his logbook. The golden egg Thule has slid into a small satchel he wears over his shoulder. "The nature of this family is thus: they ask, and people do. They are not to be questioned as to why; the answer would be a silly one. For look at all they have."

The flames begin to die down; less gristle means less chewing. "Here," Thule says. From his coat pocket he pulls a small pouch with a drawstring. "What is it?" Arnold Lovejoy asks. "His teeth," Thule says. "You left your other one in the fire."

Arnold Lovejoy falls to his knees; he retches onto the snow. "I can't imagine what that's about," Thule says. He picks up the sledge's towline. When Lovejoy has recovered, he stands and does the same.

One last image dances across windswept ice and finds its way to Arnold Lovejoy. This vision—it's a tender cat, moving on tender paws. It hops like a song from floe to floe, reaches the hut, and plays across the hot sky to his quaking brain. In it, he walks an abandoned stretch of yellow sand surrounded by an emerald sea. To his right, a stubby tree full of ripe fruit. A man made of bronze stands near the tree, guarding it. One of his daughters swims in the still water in front of him; he opens his mouth to call her but can make no sound. He recognizes a sloped hill in the distance: this is one of the beaches of Ponta Delgada.

The bronze man points to the heavens: two suns light the sky. Then darkness. He turns now and stands at the end of a long, candlelit corridor, whose walls are hung with portraits of famous whaling captains. The air smells of a ship's hold. Cutting instruments lay strewn about, wet from use. There, on the wall, he sees his own portrait. His square beard is quite distinguished; his eyes alit on some memory in the distance. It fills him with warmth to recognize himself. At the end of this hallway stand two identical doors. He feels himself watched, and understands he is being followed by something he cannot see. Through one of the doors, he knows he will find his life as he wishes it: friends, wealth, family, good meals, summer's long evenings. Through the other is gloom. But even in this dream he knows he had no way of distinguishing one door from the other. *There, there,* says one of the paintings. *It hardly matters now, does it?* He begins to cry. *What hardly matters?* But the vision now strands out of his ears like sifting fog. It will give no answer.

It's time to return.

THIRTEEN

They wait until they can wait no more, then, without speaking, anchor to the largest floe in the channel—this way, the ice will form around the *Esther,* and with luck the floes will lift the ship rather than crush her. It's the safest way to winter over.

The remaining leads are swollen with rafting ice, narrow and tight. The mate gives instructions, and the *Esther* is battened down completely. In the morning, they clear snow from deck and inspect the contact points where the ice meets the hull. Nights, the scree of the shifting, heaving ridges comes to them from a great distance away. The men, like the ship, settle into this depression. Secured and huddled below, they hear the thump of small cakes against the hull. *Knock, knock, knock.* It's like an army of patient spirits asking to be let in. But they will not be. The ice renders time and distance meaningless to the men's clocks, which, soon, will be frozen too. They construct fiefdoms underdeck: mates, cook, and cooper in steerage; seamen in the fo'c'sle. Eastman by himself.

But he stays away from the boys.

A snow squall descends on their rafted ship, and when the men emerge, they see the thick ice on the rigging no longer reflects the low light but has swallowed and flattened it. The companionways clog with drift. The *Esther's* encased sprit is hung with icicles and juts above the floes like frozen finger. It points south and seems to glow. "We should've left."

"There is no argument."

155.

"Once upon a time," says Old Sorrel . . .

He's begun leaving his nest. The boys see him swimming slowly and deliberately in the closing leads. He climbs the *Esther*'s icy hull to perch on the rail, his eyes impatiently fixed on the distance. Now and then he hovers close to the men as they work and pass time. He lays his head next to theirs; he glares at them. He opens his wide beak and shuts it behind their ears as they wait for their captain to return. But the men never see him.

His companions, the shipworms, writhe in the sea as though bathing near the *Esther*'s waterline. They bite at the ice at her hull and twist it to floating pieces. They are content to do that for hours.

"Once upon a time," Old Sorrel begins.

He is visiting the boys in their bunks. It's the first time he's talked to them in weeks.

"Perhaps there is only hope," Old Sorrel says. "Or perhaps, only hope's absence: frustration, confusion, helplessness, ringing anger. So much remains outside of one's control. One imagines a different urge. I have done this for so many years that even I am growing tired. Yet, I've set things in motion. Your captain and his friend seek an object I desire; I almost had it once, and even now, without knowing, they bring it back to me." For a time, he is silent. The boys feel the cold. "When one listens to the sea . . . and smells these rotting ships . . . It is not hard to find and follow such vessels. Sometimes, I swim away, and none aboard know I was ever there. Other times, I grow to a great height and smash them to kindling." He clacks his beak. "There is a direct line from what happens now to a world that will never be fully seen: this ice, gone; these ships, gone. I did not know who they'd send, but I knew they would send someone. It brings me joy to snip the lines I can. It's like closing a circle."

The boys are quiet. Finally, the younger one speaks. "What is it they're bringing to you?" Old Sorrel doesn't answer. "And what will you do with the *Esther*?" asks his brother. Old Sorrel shifts his weight at the end of their bunks and draws his beak to his chest. "I have not yet decided," he says. "It is the strangest thing."

And then he is quiet, too.

On the mate's orders, the men remove the darting gear and buckets from the whaleboats and outfit each with gaffs, pikes, and sheath knives; ice hooks; hand lances; an axe. The steerers strut below and return with two Sharps rifles. Two miles south, on a tongue-like floe that juts into their shrinking channel as a frozen isthmus, sleeping walrus have been seen. "Must we?" "We must." "They render so poorly." "They render." They lower two fitted whaleboats and pull south with intent in the narrowing lead.

The boys remain aboard the *Esther* with the cook and the cooper. From the crow's nest they see the large animals sleeping on the ice. They can smell them, too. At their feet, Old Sorrel sits cross-legged; he says nothing. "Why are they going so slow?" the younger boy finally asks. "If you spook one, they'll all flop," Old Sorrel says. He is not interested in the proceedings.

When the first boat reaches the crowded floe, one of the steerers scoots on his belly from the boat to the ice and lies flat so as not to startle the group. He stands slowly. A large walrus wakes; he raises his head, curious. Around him hundreds sleep. No one in the boat speaks. They are dressed in white; they move not a muscle. This enormous bull barks once. Perhaps he's their king. The steerer goes quiet and still. Another bark. *No threat,* is his announcement as he lays his whiskers and tusked head back on the ice.

Each walrus is the size of a buffalo; they snore audibly and stink of rotting fish. The steerer steps carefully—a balletic stalk, graceful, beautiful in its own way. Soon, the sleepers accept his presence, and he walks among the colony as one of their own.

With a hand signal to his boat—*be still*—he approaches the slumbering king from behind. In position, he raises and holds his rifle steady as though posing for a portrait. Then he fires a single shot into the base of the animal's skull.

The report from his rifle—blisteringly loud.

The walrus slumps as though he were a machine simply switched off. From his hairless head a single jet of dark blood squirts and pumps onto the ice. His large body quivers. He leaks quietly from his shattered brain. It is obscene. Half the walruses on the floe, startled by the shot, raise up and stretch to see what the danger is. *Where? What?* they appear to say. But the steerer has become a statue—the gun at his shoulder does not so much as tremble—and shortly the worried animals lower their heads and go back to sleep.

He shoots another bull. This time, only two or three poke their heads up in mild surprise. Whatever is making this awful sound, it doesn't concern them. Now the steerer takes aim and begins to shoot more of these dumb, resting animals. A mate joins him. They approach each sleeping beast as though patiently delivering a letter. *Bang. Crack.* The walruses—trusting creatures—have become used to the sound; they stop looking up altogether. All around them the brains and skulls of their friends and family are punctured and ruined. The shots reverberate, echo; the sound of the execution skitters across the rough range of ice and reaches those still on the *Esther*.

The animals are shot like prisoners.

Thunder, with no weather.

When the rifles get too hot, the men lower them into the water on a string; so cooled, they are soon shooting again.

The rest of the hunting party climbs from the whale-boats and the butchery begins. On the ice, they horse-piece the dead walruses, hook each with a pike, roll them over. With an axe, they chop at the porous, long tusks and stack them in piles. They chop heads from bodies and drop the heads into the ocean. They slice the animal's abdomen for its heart and liver. They throw tongues in the bottom of the boat.

Soon, nearly two hundred walruses lay dead. The pups, who have no oil, are ignored or dispatched with a knife. They swim in the bloody water at the edge of the floes and call for their mothers. Eastman and another sailor pike them for sport. The sheer amount of blood! It's astonishing. It colors and heats the ice, and the floe begins to crack audibly. The men gaff those farther from the water as the ice itself turns pink in places, dark red in others. The stain grows with each peeled carcass.

After a few hours, the men wake from their frenzy and see they have killed many more than they can butcher, let alone bring back to the ship. They finish what they can and leave the rest of the colony to rot.

Back on the *Esther*, as the walrus pieces cook down, Eastman approaches the first mate. "Will they return?" The first mate sighs. "I don't believe so." Eastman is still in his butcher's clothes. He shades his eyes and looks to the icy north. The mate matches him and remains still. In front of him, Eastman sees what he thinks to be a walrus head, its black blood dripping, hoisted. But when he blinks, he sees it's just a trick of the light. It wasn't a trick, however. It was Old Sorrel. He was trying the head on, over his own. But he couldn't make it fit.

Old Sorrel has not moved from his nest since the walrus hunt. The boys are becoming worried. "Wake up, wake up!" they say. "It's been weeks!" "I'm up, I'm up," Old Sorrel says. They pretend not to notice he's wiping tears and crust from his eyes.

162.

"I'm growing tired of this ship," he says. "And I've been thinking. Or, rather, I've been listening to my friends, the worms." He stands and rolls up his sleeping mat. "Many different rivers flow into this world. There are great rivers, one-mile broad, small ones . . . and some up to fifty miles broad and twelve miles deep. All these rivers flow along calmly. Their water is fragrant with many agreeable odors, and in them are bunches of flowers to which various jewels adhere." He clears his throat. "This is what I've been told and would like you to believe. You understand."

"Now," he continues, "the sound which issues from these great rivers is as pleasant as that of a musical instrument. It consists of hundreds of thousands of parts and, skillfully played, emits a heavenly music. It is deep, commanding, distinct, clear, pleasant to the ear, touching to the heart, delightful, sweet, and one never tires of hearing it." He holds each boy by his shoulder. They can smell the breath from his beak. It's rotten. His body is bruised.

"Those words are not mine, but perhaps you'll remember, just the same, if they are needed," he says. "I'm leaving."

The boys are upset and confused. "What are we supposed to do?" the older one asks. "Prepare," Old Sorrel says. "Steal food. Build a nest. Protect yourselves. Avoid despair. Wait." He snaps his beak. "This ship is trapped in the ice. You aren't going anywhere, but I have responsibilities. What I have to do shouldn't take me long. Keep your heads down. Mind your business." "Please stay! Without you we have no one!" The boys are crying, but they see it's no use. They are wrapped against the cold and can see their breath in the dark of the ship. He is already disappearing.

"Come, sit," he says. They do. They cross their legs and face him. "Do not depend too much on the world directly in front of you." He inhales deeply and exhales. The sound is like wind on the water. "Hold your breath," he instructs. "Imagine it now like a cap in your hand. Burrow into these planks." They do. Each feels his solitude, and in that solitude, companionship. "Don't go," the younger boy whispers. "Everything has its time," Old Sorrel says. "I will return." They stand and shake hands like formal friends. He clicks his giant beak twice and is gone.

164.

"Don't be afraid," the older boy says to his brother.

"I'm not," he replies. But of course he is. They both are. The hold is completely without light. They know he is gone. The ship feels different: it's smaller. They hear every sound the men make. "How could he?" says the younger boy. "He'll be back," says his brother. "Is this the end?" "Of course not."

There is nothing to do but believe it.

Around the *Esther*, the ice deepens; but what the men see from her rail is simply a hint of the whole, upper lips of a frozen canyon.

The floes clench and close the leads fully. The temperature drops. At first, the cold simply bites; then it latches to their skulls and won't let go. There is nothing worse for a sailor in the world than to be left shivering and trapped on the very ship that once promised unfettered movement. The thoughts encasement can conjure, the horror—it's unbearable. For who hasn't heard these winter stories? Entire fleets are crushed. No one is heard from again.

A lone survivor, who will not speak of his own survival.

Yet one night, they witness a celestial occurrence they've only heard about.

The arctic sky comes alive.

It's though someone has torn a hole in the dark firmament and sent through green and yellow waves of light to break against one another. An unseen hand pulls a shimmering curtain across the sky. It's beautiful, but it's not enough. The men have seen their passage close—they know what will happen. To hear and see the windswept Arctic is one thing; to understand it, and to sit fully in its slowly closing teeth, is another entirely. The ice cracks and pushes against itself with patient force.

Sheer canyon walls rise to surround the *Esther*.

The men slow their movements and tend to their ship in disbelief. It's as though a distant castle has raised its drawbridge directly in front of them. Inside the castle is life as they knew it. Outside, where they stand, shivering and pathetic, objects of scorn and pity, there will be no food, nor warmth, nor kindness, nor protection, nor relief. We are dead men, they think. Dead.

The cold splits them in this way and makes each man into two: one self who knows he will die right here on the ice, another who simply can't believe in that exact end. But no one has time for such wavering. Some men wake with toes black from frostbite. Others lose feeling in their cheeks. Each morning they expect to hear the sound of the *Esther*'s beam buckling from pressure. Each morning they imagine leaving her for the hostile ice. Once fully embarked across that indifferent expanse, they will turn and curse her as she crumples and sinks.

168.

The boys look everywhere. They move the barrels and bring a lamp to the *Esther*'s corners. They turn in every direction on deck, but they never see him.

The ice ramps near the ship, crinkles, sings. If he'd come to sink their ship, why has he abandoned it? It makes no sense. But then they see the way the ice has closed in on the *Esther*'s hull. It is pushing and breaking. Perhaps he cannot come back.

Perhaps he knows the ice will do the job for him.

They speak of him as one does an old friend. But is it his intention that they'd go with the ship as well? It can't be, but he isn't here to answer them. Two weeks in the ice. Three. There is no change in the weather. Activity aboard has all but ceased. They can feel their bodies losing strength. They steal the food they can.

They wish he had stayed.

And one dark morning, when they once more look for him in the *Esther*'s hold, they feel the breath of another, and see Eastman. He stands near the barrels. He's found the food they have saved; it is spread before him. "Here you are. I came down to find you. No more hiding." The boys have imagined this day and what they would do, but the sight of Eastman—he blocks out all light. Their memories return to shut off their minds. He removes his shirt and points to his own chest. "I no longer sleep. Something in me is changing."

His dark chest hair curls around his enormous nipples. His ears are black. He turns around. The scars on his back from the beating the captain had given him have almost completely healed.

They do not yell, or kick.

They freeze when he reaches for them; his cold touch roots them to the planks and they go limp. They do not protect themselves, as Old Sorrel has asked them to. For some reason, they cannot. "For the longest time, there was another boy. He let me do anything I wanted. Now he's gone."

He leaves them in a whimpering heap.

It's impossible to imagine the men aboard don't know what is happening. The *Esther* is only so big. But perhaps because their thoughts are only of themselves and the ice, or only of themselves and their probable deaths . . . "Leave them alone," the cook says afterward. But he had done nothing to stop it. His world was ending, too.

This time the boys make no effort to comfort one another. The pain does not subside. Their shame! Soon it turns to a feeling of anger whose center is everywhere and whose circumference is nowhere. It transforms in this way, and they curse the ice, and the men, and Old Sorrel for leaving them—they curse their weak bodies, their own halting breaths—and then all feeling leaves them completely. They no longer wish to be anywhere else, or see anyone else, or dream of anywhere else. Their minds have gone blank. They have no more stories to tell, except this: the ice will swallow us up.

They no longer hope for anything else.

172.

The dark days unfurl, stripped of their markings.

The *Esther* holds her men below, huddled and miserable, and notes they've stopped peering through her companionway. To the question that looms over every frozen ship as food becomes scarce, perhaps there is no answer. Thankfully, they have plenty of water. They have salt horse and walrus tongue—so they are not at that door just yet. All they see is ice and snow, and white in all directions. Will you draw straws? Will you set about the weakest and force the issue? But then, how to cook the meat?

The *Esther*'s deck brims with snow. She herself appears frozen, dressed in a gown of blanched white—but she will not be going to a fancy ball. She will stay where she is in the Chukchi Sea, with her pots filled with snow, her rigging sagged and heavy. There is nothing to be done. The ice has cooped them, bending her banded planks like shooks. The men hold themselves for warmth and fight any idea of what's to come. One may only consider the present. They are maggots, huddling in their sleeping sacks, burrowing ever more deeply into a loaf of crumbling brown bread. The *Esther* is that loaf.

173.

It is the cooper who searches for the boys and finds them topside. "Come on, boys," he says. "Come on, little orioles." They've taken off their coats and walked into the weather. By the time he spots them on the foredeck they are near death. He brings them below, and the men make space around the stove. Stepping into the cold like that—they'd done it purposefully. They called for Old Sorrel, but he hadn't come. They think perhaps they won't ever speak again. "Don't do that, boys," the men say. "Not that."

But, of course, they understand.

174.

The ice is relentless, and in time some of the men fall sick.

Those who are well keep to the galley. Those who are ill stop moving and eating altogether. Though no longer dreaming of release, they still think of the open ocean, of being fixed to a whale, lowering the cutting platform. The sound of waves licking the hull . . . They don't dare to imagine it fully. But the cold hastens, and one day, as though they have been reading of themselves in a story and hear a page crisply turned, the long nights swift away, replaced by dawn's light.

And in that dawn light, which, in its richness, has brought the healthy men topsides for the first time in a month, they see two fur-clad figures walking in the cold distance over the floes, a sledge between them.

It is the captain and Thule.

FOURTEEN

175.

During their journey home across the ice, plagued by thoughts of the *Dromo* and the image of Leander's opened body in front of him, Arnold Lovejoy had nearly convinced himself that instead of reaching the *Esther* as Thule promised, they would walk in a circle, and come upon some stitch in time: here, in the hut, he would find Leander, untouched; he would fall to his knees, beg forgiveness of some sort; they would bring him back as intended, and Lovejoy's own part in this story would remain fixed and legible to all who cared to hear it. But he'd seen what Thule'd done, and so quickly; Leander was no more. They'd burned his depot to the ground. And Thule, calm and quiet, carried the golden egg he was sent to retrieve.

He followed Thule across the ice like a chastened child, moved by heavy feet. It was irreversible. Thule looked back not at all.

And then, suddenly: the *Esther*. His frozen ship. "There." Thule has sighted the ship's bare poles as well. "Carry me home," says Lovejoy. "Oh, she will," Thule replies. On deck, Lovejoy sees a lone crewman, an arm raised in greeting. He drops Leander's pouched teeth to the snow. "He gave me no letter," he says. "Perhaps he was lying. Did he seem sound to you? Clear your fugue. Put it from your mind," advises Thule. He does. He feels no guilt now, only confusion and numbness.

He has no idea how much time had passed.

176.

From his satchel, Thule removes the golden egg and hangs it by a strap on the *Esther*'s frozen mainmast. The men watch in astonishment. Though half of them are frostbitten and rank in their gums, neither of the returning men show any signs of exposure. "Your quivering captain returns." Thule stands in front of all and presents Lovejoy to the assembled crew. "And this," he gestures to the hanging egg, "will see us home."

To Lovejoy he says: "Do you have any words for these suffering men?" "I do not." "Not one?"

Arnold Lovejoy thanks them for tending to the *Esther* in his absence. He forces a satisfied nod when he hears that her hold is now full. Once below, collapses onto his bed and falls.

It's a deep sleep, from which he very well may never return.

The men have never seen a piece of gold this size. Long after the captain and Thule have gone below, those healthy enough to be on deck stand in the cold and face the mainmast, in awe of the egg's shape and polished surface. Etched on one side is a sperm whale—his jaw open, and one could count his teeth. On the other side is a tall and hatless man. He holds a knife with one hand, and a tortoise shell with the other. Yes, they all agree. It is certainly beautiful. But there is more to it than that.

At night it shines like a lantern and bathes the deck

in calm, yellow light. In the morning, it remains free of frost. It holds a strange power and beams itself directly to them: *shhhh, shhhh, shhhh* it whispers.

It begins to heal their injured limbs. It is telling them something they already know.

Within days, the ice stretches and breaks as if waking from a long slumber. The canyon walls calve, splash tremendously, and sink; a current catches the smaller cakes and spins them in circles. Then, from the rail, the men watch in amazement as a large lead opens. It will be their passage south. "We're saved!" It is as though a pair of large hands has reached up from undersea, taken hold of their frozen lid, and pried it apart. It feels as though the earth itself were quaking open.

The *Esther* pulls anchor from the ice and hoists her sails. In no time, she travels—a strong wind blows her south through the Chukchi Sea over black water. Most of the men fallen with illness recover; they tend to the work of sailing the ship in silence. They watch the floes recede and recite a silent prayer. The ocean is alive; free of its cover, it churns and greets the sun.

Near the base of the remaining ice, which cuts, canyon-like and open, the water is green. What they are seeing is a miracle. Still, no one speaks. They spot for whale but see none. Nor do they see any walrus, swimming or peacefully asleep and dreaming.

Neither white birds nor black birds bother the sky. They hear only the whispering cut of the *Esther*'s bow through the water and the flap of her sail. As for the *Esther* herself, the golden egg has done its work. It returns her to strength—ice falls from her rigging, her sprit plunges once again. Thule had been right: it *has* opened the ice. It had saved each of them, and will see them home, for that is where it wishes to go, as well.

In the distance, the rafted floes remain implacable, white mountains against the blue sky.

When from the deck is seen nothing but flat water in every direction, the order the men have been waiting for is given—and with no small amount of joy, the *Esther's* tryworks are dismantled and her bricks tossed ceremoniously into the sea. Their work is over.

But the boys are not interested. They stand near the aft companionway and watch the men's relief without expression. They still ache from their time on the ice. Eastman shuffles among the group. They stay away.

To port, the Aleutian Islands erupt from the sea like volcanic, brown molars. The *Esther* drops her pots and sails right through. "The living ocean!" Oh, oh: relief.

Arnold Lovejoy, brought topside, watches as waves break on the *Esther*'s prow. The wind is indeed a relief; it pulls his thoughts away from where he can see them. As they sail like a weighted vision through Bristol Bay, he thinks it's possible that all of this has been a wretched dream. Perhaps he is still at the Davit Inn. Perhaps he has fallen asleep, those old riggers whispering their stories in his ear: full ship, greasy haul. The further south they get, the truer and more likely this seems, though he cannot deny Thule is near—he stands on deck and watches the water as well. He escorts Lovejoy between cabin and deck. There is no taste of rum in his mouth.

He smells the sea.

Above him, the boys sit in the crow's nest like thin birds themselves. They do not speak. And because their desire to remain silent is so strong, no one speaks to them. In the clouds that blossom behind them they see faces form and wisp away: animal faces, the face of the cook, their own. Are they alone now? It seems so.

He stands at the rail; he pays them no mind. He's been told of their attempt in the cold, a case of nerves. The danger has passed; the ice will become a memory; they will recover. The men go about their work lightly, and do not turn to them. It's understandable. The boys look terrible, drawn and frail, and what they'd done, trying to walk into the weather . . .

To worry about one's death is understandable; to invite it is not. He wouldn't want to stand near them either.

Still, a little kindness would not hurt.

The sun moves closer to the boys' skin and fills their bodies with warmth. They see no other ships as land drops from sight. From where they sit, the ocean appears wholly empty. It stretches in every direction, an embroidered shroud lain gently over the earth.

180.

Within a few days of open wind and water, all but the cooper and Eastman recover and return topside. As for those two—something has caught them on the ice that won't quickly heal or pass. They develop wet coughs and soon neither can walk or work. They stay below. One of the steerers also falls sick again, and a quarantine is set up near the fo'c'sle, where all three begin to deteriorate. As they sail away from the northern grounds, the other men begin sleeping on deck. No one wishes to catch it.

The orange sun flattens on the horizon. The ocean sweeps and expands in front of the men in a way that seems new. It's like looking at a paper lantern. The sea holds its own illumination, and moves in a patterned, decorative way. The sun itself is fixed. They can spot the brushstrokes.

The sick stay below.

181.

The boys will speak only to each other, no one else. They climb the rigging, though they are not spotting for whales. No one thinks it odd. From the hoops they imagine the ocean teeming with life; they wish it so. But they see nothing. They feel time passing. Day, day, day into night, again and again. The ice is behind them. They are aware that all of this will end—they will return to New Bedford, and then they will have to make a new life. "I'll be a cook," says the older one. "I'll work as a smith in a shop." None but they will care about their time aboard the *Esther*. That's just how it is.

But one day in the distance they spy a lone figure swimming leisurely toward them, and their hearts leap.

For he'd returned.

They meet him in the hold where his nest used to be. "What happened in *here*?" He has his net in his hands and has already begun mending it. To see him again . . . they have no words. Their anger is gone, they feel its flat surface only; but now that he's come back, they are surprised at their nervousness. They are anxious and tired. It is both a relief and not a relief to see their friend.

There is something different about him, too. For one thing, he has grown taller. For another, instead of feet like theirs, he now has talons. "I have something to show you," Old Sorrel finally says. He steps quickly to the side and with a sweeping motion, points to one of corners of the hold. The space is filled to the bulwark's brim with oil casks and bundled tusks. But there are no portholes, and the darkness is like a heavy curtain.

He snaps his fingers; a green flame appears. Now the boys see what he means: in the corner sit two bodies, water-soaked and bloated. One is missing a head; the other has suffered a great trauma to his swollen, blue face, and his mouth is stitched closed. They have been positioned stiffly with their backs against the wall, gray hands at their sides. From each leads a trail of water, as though they'd recently been dragged across the floor. "Don't be afraid," says Old Sorrel. "I had to." "Those men died months ago!" the boys cry. Old Sorrel laughs. "And now they've come back."

They are so accustomed to silence that they find they have difficulty talking at all. Once they grow numb to the bodies, however, and comfortable again in the hold, they begin to tell Old Sorrel everything he's missed—the ice and its breaking, the captain's return. They try to smile for their old friend. Then, for a long time, they sit quietly. "You can tell me anything," Old Sorrel says. Neither can quite pull the stone from his throat. "We needed you," the younger boy says. "And you left."

"Oh," says Old Sorrel. They speak slowly of Eastman, and the green light extinguishes.

He stands and approaches them. "There is darkness, and there is light," he begins. "They jostle in constant eclipse. You may find eventually that it is only through the scrim of one that the other is made visible." He takes their hands in his. "Say this hand, next to that one, next to mine. Look down. I know what I am. But what do you see? It is with hand next to hand that you might see yourself." They don't understand. "I went to retrieve these sailors from the deep. The worms said you'd be fine. I had my eye on other things." He pulls them close. They allow it to happen. His body is soft and enveloping. His arms are firm on their backs. The shipworms crawl from his beak, nestle under their legs, and they feel those as well. He smells of sweat and seaweed. "Perhaps that is not a comfort. I made a mistake. I am sorry I left you."

In the clear night sky hangs a slivered moon. But no one sees Old Sorrel as he carries the boys back to their bunks and tucks them in. No one sees as he hops up the aft companionway like a shadow and walks over the deck. He passes the men crouched at the rail. Others sit cross-legged, midship, facing the golden egg to catch its glow. Old Sorrel moves through them. He is not seen. The fo'c'sle has become a wretched place. It belches its heat toward the quarantine, where Eastman, the steerer, and the cooper lay in isolation on cots. For a second, Old Sorrel stands at the fo'c'sle companionway as though guarding it. Then he ducks his head and steps below. "Wake," he whispers to Eastman.

A strange sickness has indeed found Eastman; it attached to him on the ice and followed him here, where it's taken root and blossomed. He hasn't been sleeping. He's only been resting his eyes, which are already in great pain. Old Sorrel steps over Eastman's legs and perches on his stomach, as before. But Eastman still cannot see him.

One of the shipworms crawls from Old Sorrel's open beak and wiggles up Eastman's nose. He places his hand over Eastman's mouth. Neither the steerer nor the cooper wake. "Do not call out," Old Sorrel says. He clacks his beak once. The shipworm burrows down Eastman's throat and into his stomach. Old Sorrel makes himself as heavy as stone.

Eastman's eyes bulge. He feels his lungs being chewed. He tries to move his arms but finds he cannot. His ribs crack from the weight of Old Sorrel. Then something else does. His protruding eyes shoot their vessels; he spits up dark blood. Old Sorrel grows even heavier. A lung, punctured, gives a hiss.

Now, Old Sorrel uses both hands to compress Eastman's face. His larynx, with nowhere else to go, pops into the back of his mouth—once there it depresses his thickening tongue. Another snap and blood-gargle. Old Sorrel shifts slightly to his right and kneads one of his sharp feet atop Eastman's chest. He finds his black heart. With his talons, he scrapes and scrapes.

After some time, the shipworm crawls from Eastman's thigh and climbs back into Old Sorrel's beak. Eastman stops moving.

And that's how the thing is settled.

Up through the fo'c'sle companionway Old Sorrel hops. He passes the men again, leaps twice until he perches on the after cabin. He feels . . . it is hard to explain, even to himself. But he is not done yet. On deck, he sees the captain at the rail. He drops down the aft hatch and finds himself in steerage. Thule sits with his back to the door of his cabin, hunched over one of Ashley's charts. Old Sorrel clears his throat. "Please turn around," he says.

It is only fair. They haven't seen each other in years.

Thule recognizes the voice. He can't help himself—he grins and gloats like a cat. "I thought I'd seen you," he says, turning in his chair. "Earlier, circling the ship. What took you so long?" "I was waiting for the right time," Old Sorrel says. "Well, as you can see," Thule says, and opens his arms, "you've missed it." He is interrupted just then by a disgusting, wet sound—

Old Sorrel lunges again. This time, his great beak punctures Thule's chest completely. It sinks deep into the chart table at Thule's back with a satisfying *thunk*.

A look of surprise spreads across Thule's stricken face.

Old Sorrel churns his beak. Thule grimaces; his mouth moves but no sound finds the room. "Oh, you dumb, gleeful tourist," Thule finally says. Old Sorrel jerks and bites. Thule writhes his legs; he batters his fists on Old Sorrel's feathered head, but it is no use. Finally, Old Sorrel pulls back from the chart table and tilts his head to the ground; Thule's slick body slides down length of his beak. "Such concern," Thule says. He sits on the floor, holding his stomach—his intestines have fallen out. He is gathering them like stray paper and trying to pack them back in.

192.

"I keep waiting for you to transform," Old Sorrel says. "But for some reason, you're not." "What's the point?" Thule says. A large, stinking puddle had formed where Thule is sitting. His bones are broken. He can't stop his own spilling. Eventually he gives up. Then Old Sorrel *does* see his face change, and Thule's true features emerge. "Old age, old age," Old Sorrel says. "Those flowers are wilting. You've lost a step or two." He hands Thule a cloth. Thule takes it, folds it once. "This makes no sense," he finally says. He closes his eyes. Sweat has soaked his shirt. "You snuck aboard. But you won't win." "I'm not trying to win," Old Sorrel says. He is studying Thule intently. "I'm just here for balance." He hands Thule another cloth.

It is not taken.

"Don't gloat," says Thule. "I'll see you at the bottom of the ocean." "With luck," Old Sorrel says. He laughs and pulls the light from the room.

And then it's morning.

193.

The bodies of Eastman and Thule are wrapped and sewn in canvas, weighted at their feet, and sent over the side. Neither body has been foully played; as far as the men can tell, it is simply misfortune: an ice illness, dormant, catching up. Their faces are at peace. But to make it through this much of a voyage, only to expire so close to the end— truly a shame.

Arnold Lovejoy clears his throat. "If anyone takes even slightly sick, inform the cook." He feels as though a millstone has dropped from his neck. Thule had driven all certainty from his mind. He'd been pulled to the edge of reason.

He's relieved that he's gone.

There will be no more hunting. Without her pots, the *Esther* will sail straight and light on the ocean. He feels some part of himself returning. The *Esther* carries on her mast what Thule had drawn from Leander, and though it is clear the voyage has been a failure but for the oil and the egg, perhaps that will be enough.

The bodies of the two men fall to stern.

It is time to get home.

194.

All morning, the boys wait for Old Sorrel to appear. They look between the dark casks and the *Esther*'s stem, but the ship is empty and quiet. From the crow's nest, the lines of the sea point endlessly in every direction. The expanse is unfathomable. Perhaps they will never again see New Bedford. Under the water is more water; it stretches to the apparent horizon and rolls over. It would take nothing at all, just a small rise, for the world to be drowned. Perhaps, the boys think, it's what *has* happened while they were on the ice.

With no land in sight, the *Esther*'s movement now feels incremental.

But Eastman is gone; he will haunt them no more.

They'd watched him sink, and spat into the sea.

195.

Only the cook is greatly bothered by the deaths of Eastman and Thule. That they'd died on the same day, that's what does it; he doesn't believe in coincidence at sea. "It's the boys," he says to anyone who'll listen. "We shouldn't have brought two. It's mirror luck." But that's an old superstition; none of the other men pay him much mind. They are pleased that Thule no longer roams the deck, and to have Eastman gone, too—it unburdens their sense of what should've been done. One can't blame the boys. "Let it be," the smith says. At night, the men gather at the mainmast. There on deck, in the presence of what they've come to think of as their talisman, all seems warm and well. No matter how one turned it, the hatless man had his whale.

The golden egg has already begun its work.

F
I
F
T
E
E
N

196.

But unexpected things *do* happen occasionally.

And this is not the end for the poor *Esther* or her tired crew, and it is not quite the end of this story. For as this famous ship crosses the equator, away from the horse latitudes on her way home, the sea quiets. The wind drops, entirely; and every whistle and divot on the water smooths itself out. "Irons."

The heat lifts from the deck.

And not one man sees a wave.

The old riggers at the Davit Inn had spoken stories by candlelight to Arnold Lovejoy, but what had those stories told? Failure of the body, the folding of minds; shifting ice, how the sea handles cowards. Yet, the *Esther*'s hold is full, and with his shares he'll make a fortune. He will say what he wishes; there is no Thule to correct him. He'll say nothing of Leander. It's the wisest approach. Say they found pieces of the *Dromo*, but not him—the golden egg will be proof. He can live with what he's done. His health will return. He will buy a tall house facing the harbor, set himself up in business, where he will be welcomed. He will feel better. She will forgive him. She will not know.

On this night, the first of the *Esther*'s sudden stillness, he dreams that he himself is a whale. The pleasure he takes in his deep dives is pure and vain; it feels wonderful. He sleeps below; it's where he'll stay. *It's time to close the book*, someone whispers in his ear.

I know, he says, still in his dream. *I know.*

198.

In such unexpected calm at these latitudes, the afternoons last forever. The caught men tie canvas to the davits to ease the heat. The shade barely helps. Their first day in irons they were patient, but when they wake the third day and see their sails still hang like dirty shirts from the *Esther*'s poles, the ocean's silence fills their ears.

Their captain is below and cannot be roused. But what would one tell him, anyway? It is as though all movement has simply ceased.

Four days with no wind, thus no circulation of the air below, and the smell from the fo'c'sle grows sulfuric. They bring the steerer topsides from quarantine, lay his cot near the after house. From there he has a view of the *Esther*'s deck: dry timbers, the pin-rail leaking tar. Heat glistens the ship's planking. He sees the golden egg reflecting in the sun, and the men gathered around it.

The noon light is jumpy and the heat is a living thing: it drums atop each man's head and pushes their thoughts away.

200.

"Look, look!" The cook points. The sun, directly over-head, one can see her rings; she's been there, in the same spot, all morning. At first, the alarmed men agree that in the ocean's calm it just feels like the day is passing slowly. But soon not even the most skeptical can deny it: the sun no longer travels her wheel and, in her own stillness, hangs fixed to the heavens above them like a painted and punishing eye. The blue sea thickens. The *Esther* sails no more. And now, with neither wind nor tide, nor pitch nor sway, she begins truly to bake under the tropical, transit-less sky. Six days.

Seven.

They drink the *Esther*'s water until it's gone and, look-ing for more, find none. In desperation, they drop buck-ets over the rail and sip from the sea. Their stomachs grab at the taste; they retch and flop on the deck. They rise and pour buckets full of seawater on the *Esther*'s sprit. "Move." "Sail forth!" Nine days.

Ten.

The men gather at the golden egg fixed to the mast. It has opened the ice and seen them here—perhaps it might bring back the wind or push them through. They seek its favor. "What have we done to deserve this?" they cry to the hatless man and receive no answer. Food spoils. The smell that comes from below is like body rot. The heat pulses, ovenlike; the *Esther*'s wood wilts. Her tarring sprouts and rubs away like gums pulling back from teeth.

In time, the sun turns the men's faces brown and hard as nutshells: rutted, riveted, pit-strewn.

The silence of the sea is complete and total.

Finally, a change. "Look!"

Around the *Esther*: a grid of wavelets that crest but do not break. It must be an illusion, for there is no wind. Still, it catches their weakening attention—they simply don't know what to make of it. They watch as the ocean they can see begins to separate into small squares, delineated by these small wavelets to the horizon. Time passes. The sun does not set. They're dying. They know this.

One cannot lose all hope, and belief, in the face of such nonweather, nor during such an unheard-of lull. With the energy they have left, they beg and plead.

Yet nothing they think to offer is accepted.

"You've never asked me a single question about myself," says Old Sorrel. "That's not true," says the older boy. Old Sorrel shrugs and hands them each a cup of water. "Drink!" he says. "I saved it for you. Don't tell."

The hold smells wretched; the bodies Old Sorrel has brought aboard are still set against the barrels; they simmer and stink in the heat. The water, however, is cold and clear; it tastes like ice and calms them down. "Take a deep breath." They do. Finally, they ask if he knows why this—their sudden stillness—is happening. "It's just," Old Sorrel says, "the way I've always done things." He gestures to the corner of the hold. They see the net he's been working on is now gone.

He will not answer the rest of their questions. After they drink, he lies on his back to sleep. Feathers now cover his body in patches—they are black and long, and hang from his arms, shawl-like. He begins to snore in the heat like a bear.

"Come on," the younger boy says, and pulls his brother by the elbow. The rot smell is overwhelming. "Let him sleep." But as they make their way quietly through the dark hold to the companionway, the older boy trips over a pair of legs. He looks down. It's Eastman—blue, bloated, crushed to death. And next to him, bloodied Thule. Old Sorrel has retrieved them from the sea and returned them to the ship as well. They stink to high heaven; a pungent, fungal musk. "No!" "Don't look."

Up the companionway they go.

"Just move."

Topsides, the heat is relentless, dousing, and for a minute they are blinded by sunlight. Then they see the men: some lie around the mainmast in a circle; others sit with their backs to the rail. They lift their sunken eyes to the boys and stare. Carefully, the boys step across the shimmering deck and stand at the bow. In the distance it's impossible to see where the blue of the water meets the white of the sky; they seem to have melded into one. The sun grows her rings, they clench and seize. They produce smaller suns, ghosts they cannot blink away.

And from the bow they do see Old Sorrel's net. It floats on the surface of the sea, its knotted squares the size of salmon. And at its very center, mid-grid, sits the trapped *Esther*.

"You should've stayed below," the smith says, and turns his attention back to the egg.

202.

Arnold Lovejoy has not left his cabin; he does not visit deck. He is ill. There is nothing to be done about the overheating *Esther* and how she sits in this water, nothing he can do, nothing at all. If he is going to suffer such weather, he will do it on gimbals, in his locked room (he's bolted his door); this way, when his mind cooks, he will at least be in comfort and peace. It is his captain's right. "The sun is too close," he thinks, or says. But there's nothing he can do.

He hears small footsteps on the deck above him. Then footsteps down the companionway. *I pity the poor sailor* . . . he hums. He realizes he's forgotten the words to that as well.

203.

"I cleaned up for you," Old Sorrel says. He has covered Eastman and Thule with piece of sailcloth and cleared a space between the barrels for the boys to sit. "Sorry." Cautiously, they join him. "How are things up there?" he asks. "Not good," the younger boy says. Old Sorrel snorts. "Sorrow is the rust of the soul," he says, and gives them a piece of paper crowded with tight handwriting. The older boy hands it back. He is sweating so much he thinks he will be sick. "We can't read," he says. "We can write only our names." "Oh," says Old Sorrel. "That's no problem." He takes the paper and holds it in front of him. "Accordingly . . ." he begins.

"Accordingly, it's been said that there are eight Hells, and the door to each is opened in specificity. There is the Hell of Repetition; Black Rope Hell; Crowded Hell; Screaming Hell; Great Screaming Hell; Hell of Burning Heat," he nods, "Hell of Great Burning Heat; and the Hell of No Interval." He coughs. "That last one is open only to worms and murderers." He folds the paper, puts it in his beak, and swallows it. The boys are quiet. "The *Esther* is moving from one realm to another. It's my job to escort her. And I'm . . . never mind. It's a transfer of kingdoms." "But there's only one Hell," the younger boy says. "Oh, no," says Old Sorrel. "Who told you that?" Neither boy answers.

Old Sorrel sighs. He hands them each a cup of water and sits back on his feathered haunches. "I think you'd better trust your own eyes," he says.

Feeling faint, the boys lie down. "No, no," says Old Sorrel. He walks over and props them back up. He hands each a bailing bucket, alive with small, writhing creatures. "Teredo worms," he says. "Dug from the hull this morning." They are too hungry to decline. The worms taste rotten; their smell is unbearable. But soon one can't taste them at all. "Don't worry about saving any for *these* gentlemen." Old Sorrel gestures to the covered bodies of Eastman and Thule. "They're dead, dead, dead." He coughs and clacks his beak. "I'll get you some more water. Stay with me for a little while."

The sun is soon indescribable. She bears down on the *Esther* and widens; it is as though, rather than hanging as part of the firmament, she is an aperture that opens through it. The heat cooks the men's ears; their hair goes brittle and falls in clumps.

In their scalded minds, they see a great whale in the distance; on his hump grows an enormous tree, which grants his back shade. In this shade, a large, hawk-beaked turtle is born; he approaches their ship. Striped, black and white, he is like no creature they've seen. When they gather, nude and tired, at the rail, he turns on his shell to show his unprotected belly. He could feed all of them.

They find a dart and hand it to the strongest mate, who throws it with all remaining vigor. The iron pierces the turtle's abdomen and goes clear to his shell; he howls. But the iron draws, and he sinks into the ocean's depths like a shimmering, flippered coin. "Help us!" the men cry. No one listens, and soon they cannot move. In a final turn of the page, they wake to see a group of women moving about deck like a picking crew. They walk gingerly around the prostrate men to squeeze cold water from rags onto their parched lips.

They comb and part their greasy hair, collect their loose and falling teeth. They remind each man of his duties on land. The men recognize them, then: they are their mothers. But, too soon, they turn back into fish and re-join the sea.

The men weep for hours and hours.

The captain is visited in his cabin, too. A yellow dog leans over his useless body and looks into his eyes with great kindness. "Come back, come back!" But the dog will not stay. He climbs the companionway and swims away without a second thought.

From the very center of the ship, the boys have heard the men's weeping. "What's happening?" Old Sorrel doesn't answer. His beak is shiny and sharp; in the darkness of the hold, he clacks it open and shut. They cannot tell if he is asleep or just thinking deeply. "Are you asleep," the younger boy asks, "or just thinking?" They sit in a long silence. "Neither," comes the reply. But soon he is asleep and, curious, they creep back up into the sunlight.

The heat is blistering. It rises in waves off the ship's weeping deck. They see the men huddled, miserable, clustered around the mainmast. Some lie facedown. Their skin is crimson. Not a single one has hair. They wear no clothes at all. The boys know they are dying in each other's arms. "That's enough of that." Old Sorrel, awake now, has snuck up behind them. He places a hand on their shoulders and leads them back to the hold.

Now, in the dark, it is their turn to weep. "They're going to die!" the younger one cries. "Not yet," Old Sorrel says. "And anyway, why would you care? Did they show *you* any kindness?" The boy shakes his head. He can remember no particular kindness from the men, but still . . . He remembers the smith at his stone—the cook speaking to his pigs and chickens. He remembers Turk's head knots, and the way their stories had pitched a life shaped just for them. It has nothing to do with kindness. The death of one is the death of all. It makes no sense to Old Sorrel, but he is touched nonetheless. They ask if he can just let the ship go. He shakes his head. "Events unfold as they do regardless of how we feel about them," he says. He sits now atop a barrel marked "WH." "Here's a good one. Why fish for minnows when one is perched on the back of a whale?" he asks. To that, they have no answer.

Time slips its sheathing. In the hold, they eat and sleep; they dream, they wake; they cry, they sleep. They smell the *Esther*'s shrinking timber and her pungent oil, which leaks from the drying casks and coats the hold's floor entirely.

Old Sorrel, he's brought them water and made sure they ate. He's tried to amuse them with the strange stories of ancient times, breathing deeply; but mostly he's kept to himself. They've thought: his sadness seems to have returned.

But they wonder now if what he feels is sadness at all. His eyes are meanly set, his beak grim. He moves slowly. He picks at his nest, and drags Eastman and Thule here and there, their bodies in terrible shape. Soon they fall apart, disjoint at their shoulders, and he stops. He sulks, grows morose. He seems bored with whatever it is he is supposed to be doing. At times, he looks at the boys with what feels like an unrecognizable, deep hatred; but when he realizes they've seen his expression, he flashes his dark eyes and clacks his beak. Perhaps he is thinking deeply.

Or perhaps he spends his days lost in a memory they will never know. *You've saved us,* they want to say, but that doesn't seem right either. They don't know what to do. They wait for him to return to his normal self. The days pass in silence. They wait and wait. What they hear is only the *Esther*'s complaint; the drying of her frame; the worms burrowing her hull; the occasional fumbling and flopping of the men, on deck, slowly dying.

One day, they wake to the sound of Old Sorrel's clacking beak. Directly in front of them, he's placed the decaying Eastman. "Watch this," he says with a flourish. He pulls Eastman's body from the floor so he sits, facing them. "Are you watching?" Suddenly, Eastman's eyes open and he looks directly at them.

They freeze. They cannot get away. "Stop," the younger boy says. But Old Sorrel doesn't listen. He has his hand in Eastman's back and has begun moving him like a puppet. He shifts his weight, and Eastman's bruised right arm lifts and reached for the boys. "Stop!" they cry. With a tremendous snap of his beak, Old Sorrel snips Eastman's blue hand off at the wrist. It falls to the floor like a gasping carp; almost immediately, the stump grows another hand. Old Sorrel snips that one as well. *Snip, snip.* Each new hand reaches for them and draws closer. "No!"

212.

The cleanly severed hands form a writhing pile on the floor. The boys hold each other, horror-struck. Finally, Old Sorrel takes his hand from Eastman's back, and Eastman collapses like his cord has been cut. "I'm sorry," Old Sorrel says. He doesn't look apologetic. "I'm just passing time."

The boys say nothing.

213.

"Once more. This is interesting." Old Sorrel drags Eastman away by his feet, but pulls him closer by his shoulders. In the dim light of the hold, Eastman looks spiteful and angry.

With a flensing knife, Old Sorrel makes an incision across Eastman's forehead; he draws the blade down the center-line of his face. With a quick jerk, he peels the skin away. Where there should've been bone, the boys see only a nest of worms. They are tightly woven; they cross and go under one another. "Please stop," the younger boy whispers. "It's your favorite knot," Old Sorrel says. "Look."

They don't wish to see, but neither can close his eyes.

"I'm trying to help," Old Sorrel says, and puts the body away. "He's nothing now. He can't hurt you." "I'm going to be sick," the older boy says. He is. It's his brother who finds the piece of whale skin this time. Old Sorrel returns with two cups of water, but has nothing to say.

"I won't do that anymore," Old Sorrel says. "Forgive me. He's long gone." But seeing Eastman again, and coming for them—it's been too much. They will never forget him; they never could. His hands will find them until they are old men.

Under his scalp, a nest of worms.

"Forgive me."
But the boys say nothing.

215.

The hold grows hotter; it's infernal, dark, and in its heavy air the boys no longer wish to move. Would they have preferred the ice? It's difficult to say. But without putting it into words they begin to understand that this is the end for them: Old Sorrel has finally cast his net, and they will die aboard the *Esther*.

For some reason he hasn't told them, but that's how it is, they know, they know.

This is the practice and purpose of such stillness.

And they know.

But one day, Old Sorrel cocks his head, stands, and leaves the hold. "I have a present for you," he says when he returns.

He bows and steps aside. Standing behind him, looking thin and terrified, stands Arnold Lovejoy.

Despite the heat, their captain wears galoshes and his best woolen jacket. He shakes from head to toe. "Can he see you, too?" "He can now, but I look different to him," says Old Sorrel. "He's quite sick. I asked him to dress up." "How come?" the younger boy says. He feels as though he is asleep and having trouble waking. He wipes salt from where it's crusted near his eyes. Old Sorrel claps his hands and rubs them together. In the dark a small light begins to glow and pulse. Then he shows his hands to the boys as if to reassure them he holds nothing and is not playing a trick.

"Because," he says, "you are leaving."

Together, they step over the bodies of Eastman and Thule, dodge the leaking casks. Old Sorrel leads them to the companionway, then moves to address the boys and their captain. "Don't be alarmed." He turns and hoists himself into the light.

They are greeted with an expected sight: though the *Esther*'s deck is the same—they see her mainmast and the midship shelter, the main hatch, the fife rail—the men are nowhere about. They've disappeared. In their place, the boys see that the deck is swarming with clusters of red and black crabs. They move with their claws held angrily in the air and skitter sideways over the *Esther*'s planking on pointed, tapping legs. Below the *Esther*'s bell, two crabs tentatively circle one another, their mouths clicking and wet. "Bless my soul." Old Sorrel chuckles.

Between them, one of these crabs has flipped onto his back. He cannot turn himself over. He pedals his sharp legs frantically in the air, his white belly exposed to the sun. His effort draws attention, and in no time he is descended upon by three others, who use their claws delicately to snip at his circling legs. Together, they pull the rear two legs from his body, puncture his soft carapace, and begin to peel his under-shell with their pincers. As they dig and tug the morsels from his belly, the set-upon crab churns his legs more slowly; he's out of steam. Then his legs seize on their joints; he releases a string of spit and succumbs. The feast continues. "There are your old friends," Old Sorrel says to the captain, and signals to the clattering deck. Arnold Lovejoy is sweating profusely. "Not my friends," he finally says. "Just my crew."

With careful steps, they follow Old Sorrel across the deck. Crabs scatter about their feet, seeking shelter; some climb the rigging; others scooch and hide under the windlass. Near midship, the boys see a cluster of about twenty; they are gathered around the mainmast. *This* is a docile group—no fighting, no posturing. In fact, despite their opening and closing mouths, there is very little movement at all. "It's all they can think about," Old Sorrel says, and points to Thule's golden egg.

The crabs do seem to be gazing up at the mainmast in rapt attention. Each has aligned himself to maximally face the mast; each leans slightly back, eye-stems still. Some hold their claws to the sky like open flowers and remain perfectly motionless.

The golden egg *is* beautiful, and it *does* glint in the sun.

It *does* make you want to look at it, the boys think. It's been hung there on its necklace like time itself.

"Don't stare," says Old Sorrel. He leads them midship, to the mainmast, then signals stop. He alone tiptoes through the motionless, clawful congregation and then, in one quick motion, removes the nail from the mainmast and holds the necklace aloft. The crabs watch with curiosity as he brings it to the boys. "Here," he says, and gently loops it over the head of the younger. The air fills with wet, clicking sounds. "What's this for?" the boy asks. Old Sorrel thinks long and hard. "You," he says. "And you. It's all right. Take it with you. Keep it safe in your passage and it'll carry you home."

The egg is heavy on the younger boy's chest, still warm. He's confused. "But don't you want it? Isn't this why you came?"

"Yes, it was. At first."

"And now?"

Old Sorrel snaps his beak once more. "Things change," he says. "Just look at your poor old friends." He arches his back to look directly at the sun. "Don't think on it too much. You needed me, and I left. But now you must take care of each other." He rests his hand on the younger boy's shoulder. "You can trust me. And anyway, how else will you get back?"

The boys don't know what to say.

"Then say nothing," Old Sorrel says. "It's time. I'm going to snip these lines. It's what I came to do."

The crabs have watched this scene with interest; now they begin to snap their claws in the air like furious castanets. They spit on the deck and climb all over one another in attempt to reach the younger boy. Old Sorrel blocks their path. They snip at his bare ankles, but it has no effect. In anger, they begin climbing the rigging. "Better lower," says Old Sorrel. "The waist boat is ready. They want that back." One enormous crab climbs the yardarm above them, and as they ready the whaleboat, he cries and drops like a stone with his pincers out. Old Sorrel leaps and, in his beak, catches the bomber midair, and with a flick of his feathered head, tosses him high. The crab flips twice, stripped of all dignity; then he falls directly into Old Sorrel's wide gullet, and is swallowed whole.

As the lowered hull of their waist boat touches the water, they see a lead open in front of them—a break in the strange netting, a patch to the sea from the ship. "Go!" Old Sorrel shouts. And with their sick captain in his thick woolen jacket, they pull away.

"Grab an oar, please," Arnold Lovejoy says. Chin down, he rows as hard and fast as he can. The boys sit in the stern and face the *Esther*. They can see Old Sorrel on deck—he is spearing crabs with his beak and flinging them into the ocean.

When they are a quarter mile away from the *Esther*, when it feels as though their wasted arms are numb from rowing, they are startled by a sound like a tree splitting. They drop their oars. It's Old Sorrel—they can see through a break in the *Esther*'s rail that he's begun to quiver and shake. He falls to one knee. The crabs swarm over his body and begin pulling at his feathered head. "Go back!" the younger boy shouts, but Lovejoy will not move.

They watch from their small boat as Old Sorrel stands and grows to the size of a giant. His feathers are black as tar; they cannot see his eyes. His silver beak glints in the sun; the crabs tumble from his shoulders to the deck. He is as tall as the yardarm. He is growing still. Another loud crack. It is the sound of the *Esther*, breaking apart.

Their old friend, enormous now, bends over the rail. He dips his beak in the water and takes a long drink from the sea. "What's he doing?" the older boy says. His brother cups the egg with his hands. "I don't know." Old Sorrel rights himself and lets the sea fall from his open mouth. The sound is like surf in a cavern. Then he looks once to the boys, returns his hands to the *Esther*'s masts, and snaps them like breadsticks.

The *Esther* buckles midship where Old Sorrel has straddled her; she splits right in half. Then, it is as though the sea itself begins to crumple her beam. From her hold, barrels pop to the surface like old, wooden buoys. The sun blinks once as the ocean grasps her ship. And then the *Esther*, her cargo, her crew, and Old Sorrel, who had been their protector, and who had known and cared for them, who had come when they needed him and who had lived alone in darkness for months and months—

All of it—every bit—sinks below the surface completely.

Where the *Esther* had been there is not so much as a divot in the sea. No piece of floating wood; no debris of any sort. "Well." Arnold Lovejoy looks stricken. He feels his throat completely closed up. "She buckled faster than I would've thought. That's all I want to say about it." "She survived the ice," the older boy says. Arnold Lovejoy nods. The boy is clearly trying to make him feel better, but he feels nothing at all.

That's imprecise. Perhaps it would be more accurate to say he feels stretched thin; perhaps as though he sits atop the head of a pin; perhaps hung over a chasm where feeling is obliterated altogether. Such a narrow handhold. For who was the figure who'd come to his cabin, and escorted him to the boys . . . even in the heat, he wore skins, his face snow-covered . . . had helped him into his jacket, and into his boots . . . "I recognize you," he'd said, but it wasn't entirely true. Yet he knew it was the man who'd begun his story, who'd found him on the ice, handed over his letter, and sent him to the Ashleys.

To be dangling like this! The man's eyes were gleeful and satisfied, the darkest black. He took his hand and lead him to the *Esther*'s quivering hold. Arnold Lovejoy! Singular fool. He releases his hold now and feels the pull in his stomach.

For a second, he imagines he is a bird himself, soaring overhead. He sees their tiny whaleboat, he in his red coat near the stern; he sees the boys in the bow; they three the only survivors of the wreck of the whaleship *Esther*. There is no way to look at it except directly: he's played his strange part, and now it's over. His ship is lost, and they are discarded. They float, unprotected, in a whaleboat on the wide, wide sea.

And as for Old Sorrel: his net is no more. The sun goes down—she buries herself below the horizon, relieved and extinguished. The wind picks up and their small whaleboat is lifted by a gentle swell.

The interval is over.

S I X T E E N

221.

What dreams visit such survivors? When one does not know what he has seen versus what he's already dreamed, perhaps the rustling sound of the sea comes back to his ears, and perhaps the smell of salt air . . . perhaps it's settling. Perhaps the waves hand them back and forth, one on his back in the small boat, the other two huddled to stern.

One hears about marooned men dreaming of fancy balls as the clock strikes twelve; one hears of explorers telling others of their time on the ice: this happened, then this, then *this*. One knows the ocean resumes herself to even out after all but the most reckless events; an unseen hand pulls a sheet over a bed; a child tucked in is rocked softly. There is relief in being alive. The night is hot and clean, the sky above deep, infinite, dark. The stars themselves are like spilled milk.

Exhausted, they sleep.

There will be the question of food—the salt horse they have, which they found tucked in their captain's jacket pocket, will not last very long.

Perhaps soon they will see a passing ship, maybe soon they will find themselves in a well-traveled lane. . .

They drift south.

Days pass.

When it rains, the boys collect water in the bailing barrel and mainline tub. They catch two fish, and share one with the captain, who's grown silent, unwilling, or unable, to move. He lies in the stern, watching the water. He turns occasionally to face the sky. They tell him of the worms in the *Esther*'s planking, of the sharks disappearing from view. They speak of their first whale, and baleen they stacked. More days, more nights. A welcome, warm evening current attaches herself to their whaleboat—movement without movement.

Their little whaleboat, a cork in the sea.

222.

Within a week, they see in their captain's eyes that his end is near. He is gravely ill. He sweats through his woolen jacket yet refuses to take it off; he smells like an old, scared sheep and rests his head against the stern seat. He will not take food. His lips have cracked, and his face is red from the sun. "Here." They stretch the canvas so its shade covers his face. They dip their fingers in the rain bucket, and paint water across his lips. "It's no use." "Still."

At night they hold him and speak to him in the way they know how.

223.

With sail down, no wind, they drift. One day folds into another, another, and like that time passes. The younger boy cradles the captain while the other sets his fishing line. They eat in silence. One morning, his breathing is labored—the breaths themselves are like wind rasping through dry grass. His eyes bulge and relax. It's time. "There, there," they say, for now he looks like one of the men Old Sorrel had kept in the hold. "There, there." The repetition, it's like a winding down. They can think of nothing else of comfort to say.

His mind is a punctured shell shot through with image. There is an orca whale, swimming with her young. There is a funny-looking bear, saluting him. Then he is at home, in his daughters' room. He is trying to tell them something. His wife listens through the door.

He clears his throat and looks at the boys. "What will you eat?" It's not what he'd meant to say, just what's come out. His eyes bulge once more, as though for luck; he strains at his neck. Then, with a snapping sound that comes from the very back of his open mouth, he expires.

With some difficulty, they roll him over the side and watch him sink. The afternoon sun beats upon their heads. They stretch more canvas across the bow and tuck their legs into the shade. The only sound they hear is the licking and sucking of wavelets breaking on the whaleboat's thin hull. *Now,* they think, fearfully, *we are entirely alone.*

But they have each other. And though the days are hot and the food is scarce, though their eyes have become crusted with salt and their gums have begun to soften, they keep company with all the sleek and clumsy creatures in the ocean. The water is clear, but they cannot see to the bottom. When they try, they see only a blue darkness, and depths they can only dream of—an absence of color, of all light, of warmth. But whale, squid, sunfish, tuna, krill, sharks: they are all there somewhere. The sea is their mother. She cradles them in their cedar-planked boat like the boys they had once been. The days are flattened by light. The nights are cool and deep, then soften as the morning comes on. They connect one star to another: there, there, there. Crab, bird, shipworm, porpoise, whale.

224.

They look for Old Sorrel in the water, but he never comes. They search for his face in the clouds, his face never forms. They wait in the tarped bow of their whaleboat, as they endure sudden rain and thunder; they swim off the stern and as far away from their boat as they dare; they recount what Eastman had done to them, in the dark of the *Esther*. They speak to their egg and slap their thinning bodies and scream *if you don't come rescue us right now* but one day moves into the next and he will not appear. It's for the best. He'd been kind to them, but they'd also seen him as the *Esther* sunk: he'd smashed her to bits, killing everyone aboard. He'd never been happier. It *was* for the best. It was *for* the best. They don't know quite how to say it. But it is.

But one morning near the end, they see Old Sorrel has indeed returned to them. He perches on the stern, fastidiously cleaning his feathers. He's been watching them sleep for quite a while. They are sick, now, delirious from the sun, dull from hunger. Just the same, they are overcome with happiness to see him again. "You're back!" They try to climb toward him. "Don't move!" he says and holds out his hand. They are confused. Why come at all? But then they see why he's stopped them. There, uncomfortably settled in the stern between the maid's head and pike pole, directly in front of where they had slept, is a crab the size of a dog. "Hold tight," Old Sorrel says.

The enormous crab is red and brown, his pointed legs go *thock-thock-click click-thock click* on the hull; his black eyes twirl on their stems. Out of his mouth he blows a stream of spit bubbles—these are incandescent; they bunch and hang from his mandibles like grapes. In one claw, held aloft as though in greeting, he grips the captain's woolen jacket. "Oh, no," the older boy says. "Give him a second," Old Sorrel says. Neither boy moves. It is like . . . they have no idea. They've never seen a crab this size. He batters the side of the whaleboat once with his claw, then shuffles his legs and settles back down. "Is that him?" the younger boy says. "It is," says Old Sorrel, and laughs. They look at the captain's pale, plated stomach. There is no recognition in his eyes, just a crustacean's blank, black stupidity. He spits again. Then he sits down and raises his claws. He's looking at the younger boy; the egg hung around his neck has begun to glow.

"What an idiot," says Old Sorrel.

The boys are happy to see their friend. They tell him of their time in the whaleboat with the captain, of drinking rainwater to stay alive. Old Sorrel nods gallantly. They notice his body has changed—he no longer has talons, and his bruises are gone. In fact, his body is exactly as they'd seen it the first time—young, smooth, unblemished. They tell him of the constellations they've named and the fear they've felt. He listens with interest. But soon they find they have nothing more to say. "That's all right," says Old Sorrel. "I'm just dropping by." In the silence that follows, the younger pulls the egg from around his neck, and they stare at the hatless man etched on its surface. Awkwardly, he tries to hand it to their old companion. "Please," the younger boy says. "We don't want this anymore. It's yours." But Old Sorrel shuts his beak, shakes his head. "It takes you home, now. It'll carry you to shore." His eyes have grown softer, somehow. "I've discovered I can wait," he says. "I sank my ship. I am happy. And I have nothing but time!" Their small whaleboat lifts on the swell. Old Sorrel studies them closely. "Don't look at it too much, and give it to the man who wants it most. I had something else I wanted to tell you," he finally says, "but now I can't for the life of me remember what it was." "That's alright," the boys say. "So much is lost," he says. "Sometimes I lose track."

"That's all right," they say once more.

Then, as though his own forgetfulness was a cue of some sort, he suddenly stands and stretches tall on the whaleboat's rail. He opens and closes his great beak, gives a cry, and then, with tremendous speed and finality, brings his beak's pointed tip down like an awl directly through the very center of the captain's shell. The captain doesn't know what to do. He can't reach Old Sorrel with his claws, though he tries. Brown liquid, his own, sloshes to the bottom of the whaleboat. His legs clatter about like a maraca from hell. The pain he feels is great; in it, perhaps, he can still find some strength to wrench himself free.

But once Old Sorrel begins stirring and churning with his beak, it's curtains. His vision goes black; soon he is only a twitching pile of meat and shell at the bottom of a boat and cannot imagine himself as anything else in the world.

When he quiets, Old Sorrel leaps gingerly off the rail and grabs the lip of the captain's shell through its eye sockets; with a grunt, he tears the top of it clean off. The captain's white meat and hollow-tubed sinew glisten in the hot sun. "Eat, eat!" he says, tossing the shell over the side. "You've gotten so thin!" Then he disappears, truly for the last time.

PART
THREE

Rescue at Sea, The Crossing of the Plains, New Bedford,

A Final Parting of the Waves, Timbo's Return

\\\

1880

Once in New Bedford, the boys are dropped off near the wharves. They see ships like the *Esther* heaved over, in the process of being stripped and resheathed with copper; foul men bark orders at smaller men; two cats fight over a fish some bird had dropped. A swaying bosun's mate with sour breath invites the two of them into the Yorkshire Pit, signaling them with a rum-wave; they decline. Everyone knows of their rescue. It is the talk of the town. The older boy checks a piece of paper in his pocket; he asks a passing horseman for directions. The horseman points north. Up the hill they go.

The ship that rescued them was a luxury steamer named *The Empress*; she'd been on her way from Panama to San Francisco when bad weather knocked her off course; when the weather cleared and the waves stopped capping, a steward on the shuffleboard deck spied through binoculars a ratty whaleboat, tipping on the swell. His binoculars were a new model, one which used Porro prisms; he wasn't sure of the technology, or if he'd seen anything at all. He called one of the guests over. Sure enough!

They'd raised the alarm. All aboard were surprised to find two boys in the boat—two boys who were, barring severe exhaustion and mild exposure, in good shape to boot. Their rescue was the sensation of the trip. Their needs were seen to. After a bout of poking and prodding, the ship's doctor mandated five days of complete rest and the pampering began: they were invited to dinner every night, asked to dance; they were passed from family to family. They tried to speak of what happened aboard the *Esther*, but found, when they tried, they could not. Nothing made sense in retrospect. Everyone understood.

As news of their rescue spread, Ashley himself arranged train passage for the two of them. *Had they brought anything back?* his letter asked. Through one of the men they'd met aboard *The Empress*, a lawyer who could both read *and* write, they answered: *Yes.* Through the train window all sorts of images found them: huge, snow-peaked moun-

tains; an expanse of red desert; a brown river which had
flooded its muddy banks, whose rush was momentarily
louder than the train's engine. Field upon field. The coun-
try opened itself up to them. The land—it was a golden
ocean; they rode right through.

That they were the only ones who'd survived the sinking of the whaleship *Esther*—it boggled the mind. And
that they would speak of it to no one who asked . . . well,
it was understandable to the people who knew of them
and approached on the train. They took their meals in silence in the dining car, and only occasionally left their
sleeping room, for it had a wide window they'd come to
love. There was no need for them to linger on the obser-
vation deck.

Ashley had arranged it.

At first they saw Old Sorrel everywhere—in the red hills
of Utah, and in the textured cornfields of Iowa. Once, in
the sudden darkness of a rock-bored, stone-lined tunnel,
they caught him in the window's reflection. But his ap-
pearances grew fleeting, and when they spoke to him,
he never answered. At night, the younger boy pulled
the golden egg from under his shirt and hung it in their
cabin. It swung like a lantern and lit their lonely car as it
rumbled toward New Bedford.

The old woman answering the Ashley's door looks like a gruff walrus herself. "Children!" she exclaims. "This is the way, step inside." She leads them into large living room, painted white. Sitting there expectantly they see Ashley and his wife. On the walls of this great room, they see oil paintings that depict various whaling expeditions. *The Closing Floes; The Skinning of the Walrus; Encounters with the Esquimaux; A Fall from the Rigging; The Melting Ice; No Wind.* Without delay, Ashley stands and takes the necklace from the younger boy—he pulls it right from his neck as though plucking an apple from a tree. "There she is," he says. He holds the golden egg in front of him and turns it in the firelight.

"What is it?" the older boy says. "Don't be stupid," he replies. "It's what brought you here to me."

"Have some sympathy, dear," Mrs. Ashley says.

Ashley coughs. "I'm sorry, this . . . it's important to my family," he says. "And to my business. I'm rebuilding the *Dromo*. And this . . . this assures continuity. It confers it, if you will. We've carried this egg like a book in our hands for generations. I've waited a long time to have it back." Mrs. Ashley leans forward in her chair. "Perhaps," she says, "it's simpler to say that he took something that wasn't his, and it's a relief to have it returned."

"Yes," Ashley says. "That."

233.

A bell rings and a meager lunch of fried smelt, dry cheese, and crackers is served. The boys sit as politely as they know how. When they are asked to tell the story of the *Esther,* and how she came to her tragic end, they do the best they can. They are delicate with detail, and hesitant at first, but they leave nothing out. "Oh, dear," Mrs. Ashley finally says. "It sounds like you've had quite a fright," says Ashley. "Of course they're upset," says Mrs. Ashley. "They have no mother, and everyone they know is now dead. They were drifting in that little dinghy for *months.*" Ashley tosses a handful of smelt into his small mouth. "Did you eat anyone?" he says.

There is a gasp. But the boys don't know where it's come from. It's as though it sounded from behind the dark curtains in the far corner of the room.

Ashley takes another handful of smelt and makes short work of them. Then he hops off his chair. He walks until he is within darting distance of the boys and clears his throat.

"I can tell you are in distress," he says. "In this room. In this house. But these stories are old and one ought to take comfort as actors who have played a part in something that has gone on for years and years. The particulars may not make sense, but the story, which takes longer to tell, will, in time, make itself legible. Time means nothing to you, you are . . . too young. But any pain you feel will leave you, and it will be replaced by something else, and I hope you will allow the following words to be of comfort."

And then, reciting from memory, he begins.

"It is true that life is fleeting and full of discomfort, but we will convene in the end, and there we shall meet with thousands and thousands. There we shall see our elders and our sons, our friends, our mothers. There we shall see angels with their golden harps, and men, who in this world were cut into pieces, burnt in flames, eaten by beasts, and drowned in the seas for all the love that they bore to the Lord of this place." He opens his eyes and looks closely at the boys. "They have not left us. They are all well and clothed with immortality as with a garment." The old woman has again come through the door, and now stands there listening. Ashley closes his yellowing eyes. His voice has fluttered around the darkened room like small bat, and now it's come to rest.

"Mr. Ashley," Mrs. Ashley says. "I haven't heard that in a while. I'd thought that hand amputated years ago." Pleased by the sharpness of his old mind, Ashley wipes a tear from the tip of his nose. "It's a tragic story. The ship, the men. The loss is . . . immeasurable," he says now to the boys. He clasps each on his shoulder. "One may re-call the Slough of Despond—it is why I, myself, no longer embark on the sea. There is nothing there for me. Yet the whale has not *yet* been eradicated. There is still more to squeeze." The boys smell his breath. They see his sharp teeth. They wish, suddenly, to be anywhere else. "It is why I send others. It is," Ashley says, "the cost of doing business."

"But what about the beasts themselves?" Mrs. Ashley says.

She's stood from her chair and now closes on the boys as well. During lunch, her hair had come loose from its bun, and hangs now in strands like gray weeds around her ears. "Do *they* not object?" "Ah, yes," Ashley says, and turns to his wife. "The Providence of God is manifested in the tameness and timidity of these creatures." Ashley coughs, spits, and continues. "And whereby they fall victims to the prowess of man, and are rendered subservient to his convenience in life . . ." He clears his throat. "That they cannot speak, nor answer back; it's in their design. Their suffering is theirs alone. It's unheard. And to it I offer neither consolation nor embrace."

The old woman who'd seen them in now bursts out in applause. "Oh, oh," she cries, beside herself. This is an old game. One the boys suspect has very little to do with them. "We'd offer you dessert," Mrs. Ashley says, "but you boys have clearly eaten enough."

The afternoon comes to an unceremonious close, as Ashley gives them no money for their non-lays of the *Esther*'s lost oil. For the safe delivery the necklace, and for carrying home his golden egg—for enduring the long passages and the ice and the heat, for being active and complicit in the slaughter of the whale while not being cowed by the ocean, for falling prey neither to superstition nor the sea's indifference, in acknowledgement of the hardship faced when growing up without a mother in this day and age, and in recompense for seeing and experiencing things no child should ever have to at the hands of the sea, Ashley pulls a single-flued harpoon from his collection. He hands it to them as though it were God's child himself.

"It's an heirloom," he says, and sends them on their way.

They know nothing of the woman who'd stood behind the curtains during lunch. They know nothing of the letter she's received, nor what she's seen of their ship, nor the murmur it's caused her heart. They do not know of her regret, nor of her understanding of her family. They do not know her unhappiness, nor of the egg's warping power. They know nothing of her child. But they do know, when she catches up with them near the docks and asks for a word, that she is an Ashley. She wears the same black dress as the woman who'd seen them in. Her hair is worn exactly like her mother's, and she has her father's eyes—but she is young and beautiful.

"I heard everything," she tells them.

237.

People on the street stop to look. Over her shoulder, the boys see a large, mangy dog, watching them from the bushes. "Will you go to sea again?" she asks. The older boy shakes his head. "That's right," she says. She asks about Arnold Lovejoy and his end; they tell her the truth. She asks about the *Esther* and where they slept while aboard. She hands each a brooch in the shape of a bird. It is gold, with ivory inlay. "I am so sorry," she tells them. "You were so very brave."

Her own child is now five years old. He'd been asleep in his old nursery as they ate, the golden egg already draped around his sour neck. "Hello," someone is saying to him, even now. "Hello, beautiful boy." He will heal and grow up to be a vile and powerful creature. He will pursue his vain profit, pull from the world, and we will all be the worse for it. But that's another story altogether.

For now, in the middle of the street, Sarah Ashley wraps the brothers in her arms, and whispers in their ears. Then she stands. For a long time, no one says a thing. "That's all," she finally says, and they turn from her to go.

She watches the two boys walk slowly down the waterfront.

She watches as they put the brooches in their pockets. The taller boy places his arm around his brother's shoulders. Not a single person pays them any mind. The leads had opened, and now they've closed. In front of her now is just the street—the loud shopkeepers, the wagon-pushers, the ships and the ship-smell. She is bereft.

Finally, she turns to make her way back up the hill to where her house, with its scowling face and heavy door, and its large windows angled toward the wharf, where her father and mother now sit with her brothers and her child, and a full library of leather-bound books that sing of all the New Bedford Ashleys have done and seen . . . and their charts and their candles, which give off the most perfect and odorless light. The log in which Arnold Love-joy's name has been written is now shelved, his name a footnote along with Leander's, and Thule's. There will be the empty dining room, and some uneaten smelt, all of it waiting for her.

A last detail of this parting is worth mentioning. Once she is out of sight, from the bushes behind where Sarah Ashley had stood bursts the old dog—he has watched the entire scene unfold. It's Timbo, still alive after all these years. He'd seen them off, and now he's seen them return. He has no tail, and his fur is a little worse for wear, but neither stick nor string trails behind him, and he is free. He sniffs once at the busy street, twice. All is quiet, all is still, chirp the birds gayly. Then he runs after the boys, as though there is one more thing he wishes to tell them.

240.

Returned now from the *Esther* to the stream of time, the boys grow up. They marry well, and have children, and in time those children have children of their own. They remain, for the entirety of their lives, in New Bedford. The town grows and changes, thrives and crumbles; they keep to themselves. Neither manages to find fulfilling work, it is either too hard or it pays too little, and they are embarrassed by impersonal slights. They are impatient with the people who love them and are quick to find fault in others. But soon even these regrets don't matter. Time solves them. And in their later years they often think how strange it is that, looking back on their lives, they can no longer pinpoint the exact moment when familial joy turned into happiness, and happiness, as they moved into the periphery, changed quietly into something else.

They never speak of their sadness to one another or mention the porousness of their certainty; they never speak of the awe in which each has held the other's resilience, nor the admiration each has felt in presence of the other as he's made his way through the dark and denuded world without bending to it fully. They don't speak of Old Sorrel. The sinking of the whaleship *Esther* is not a story they tell often. It never comes out quite right. Time passes and soon no one wants to hear it at all.

It is strange. In their old age, they often feel as though the world can barely tolerate them. Just die already! everything seems to say.

241.

But who can forget the smell of the freshly cut shooks, and the salt-grit of the wind? And the sound of the blacksmith, sharpening darts at his stone? They'd seen neither tameness nor timidity in the great creatures they'd sought. They'd seen mothers care for their young, enraged by their slaughter. In their drifting boat they'd collected rainwater, picked crab-shells clean, and felt their strength return. They'd watched the waves grow in height and sledded down each wave's trough.

In the tarped bow of their whaleboat, they'd sung to one another for company. They'd placed hand next to hand and watched the water turn amber and then wash back to blue. Who can forget the horrible Eastman and his foul breath, or the captain's stupid woolen coat? Or their first glimpse of *The Empress* and her steam stacks?

Who can forget the cook and his pig? Or the call of the mate, as the waves crested the *Esther*'s bow, singing *eyes up, eyes up, eyes up*? For a while, when they sleep, they dream of fish that glow in the depths, diatoms constellated like stars, and a sperm whale arching his clumsy back to swim straight down. And who can forget that they'd had one another? Not them.

Not them in the least.

END

AUTHOR'S NOTE, PART II

No ship trims her own sails, and so for their support and encouragement, I'd like to thank my colleagues at Trinity College, in particular Chloe Wheatley, Ciaran Berry, and Clare Rossini. My uncle, Bill Mayher, for his love of the sea. My parents. Anne Hanley, for keeping Alaska on my mind. Peter Murray, for writing such beautiful music. Matt Burgess and Paul Yoon, for their sharp, insightful reads and constant companionship. My teachers Jim Shepard, Charles Baxter, and Julie Schumacher. Will Evans and the entire crew at Deep Vellum / A Strange Object. Sarah Burnes for being amazing.

And, of course, Jill Meyers. I feel so lucky.

To Maryhope, Llewellyn, and Alistair, *true* legends of the sea: enduring gratitude and love with no horizon in sight. You've made home our own small ship—stronger, happier, and just plain old *more fun* than anything I could've imagined.

ABOUT THE AUTHOR

Ethan Rutherford is the author of two story collections—*Farthest South* and *The Peripatetic Coffin and Other Stories*—and for these works has been named a finalist for the Los Angeles Times Art Seidenbaum Award for First Fiction, a finalist for the John Leonard Prize and CLMP's Firecracker Award, received honorable mention for the PEN/Hemingway Award, was a Barnes & Noble Discover Great New Writers selection, and was the winner of a Minnesota Book Award. Born in Seattle, Washington, he received his MFA in creative writing from the University of Minnesota and now teaches creative writing at Trinity College. He lives in Hartford, Connecticut, with his wife and two children.

North Sun, or the Voyage of the Whaleship Esther is his first novel.

ABOUT A STRANGE OBJECT

Founded in 2012 in Austin, Texas, A Strange Object champions debuts, daring writing, and striking design across all platforms. The press became part of Deep Vellum in 2019, where it carries on its editorial vision via its eponymous imprint. A Strange Object's titles are distributed by Consortium.

**This printing of *North Sun* is made possible by
the generous support of:**

Adam Brennan
Kristin and Ryan Boyd
Sarah Burnes
Calvoz & Cordon
Tony Rhorer
Ron Restrepo
Cullen Schaar
Roslyn Dawson Thompson and Rex Thompson
Ben Fountain
Mark Perkins
Jane Saginaw Lerer and Stephen Lerer

www.ingramcontent.com/pod-product-compliance
Lightning Source LLC
Chambersburg PA
CBHW021953130726
47903CB00014B/1278